I0628867

Second Chances

Written by:

Aaron D. Brinker

Copyright © 2017 Aaron D. Brinker

Cover art by:

The Book Khaleesi

www.thebookkhaleesi.com

Chapter 1

Chaun Hutchins lived a common life. He had earned his degree, got a job in his field of study, was married, and had a child on the way. The area of his life that placed him with a silent minority, was the verbal abuse inflicted by his wife Katrina. Chaun had no idea that, within the next two hours, his life would drastically be changed.

It was a cold night in December. That winter had remained dry. No rain, no ice, only bitter cold. He and Katrina, were at a party, and she was talking with her best friend Shannon Billings. Chaun stood off to the side of the room alone. He was usually personable and outgoing, but lately he was reserved and very distant from most. He watched as his best friend, Jake, approached him. Jake Billings was Shannon's older brother and the host of the party. "Chaun, you all right?"

"Yeah. Why do you ask?"

"You don't seem like yourself tonight. Usually you're out talking with everyone and getting people laughing. You just seem quieter than usual."

"I'm just focused on the new exhibit opening at the museum this week, that's all. It's been in the works for a long time." He fidgeted with the glass he was holding, nervously, running his index finger back and forth along its lip. "I've been getting sick of how Kat's been treating me lately as well. I know most of it is hormonal issues with her being pregnant and all, but it still gets to me from time to time."

"I can't imagine trying to deal with all of that at once. Honestly, I know there were times when she wasn't pregnant that she would treat you like dirt. Granted she has a good heart and all, but a good portion of the time she can come off as very abrasive."

"That is true. I've just gotten fed up with it lately." His head lowered as he looked at the glass in his hand. "Maybe if I wait until after the baby is born things will ease up a bit. Like I said, with the hormones going crazy right now it could be making it worse."

Jake placed his hand on Chaun's shoulder. Chaun raised his head slightly looking at Jake. "You might have a point. At least get out and start acting like your old self. Everything at work will be fine. You've handled it many times before; this time should be just like all the rest. Worry about it while you're at work and not my

3

party. You should be having fun and not standing in a corner feeling sorry for yourself."

Chaun gave a slight smile, "Maybe you're right. I'm usually the life of the party. You've always said I typically am like your party's court jester. Got to admit though… there are a lot of easy targets here tonight. Look at all these crappy sweaters. I feel like I'm at a damn convention of grandkids with cheesy Christmas gifts."

Jake started laughing, "That's more like the Chaun that graces my parties with his presence. Get your ass out there and have some fun."

On the other side of the room, Katrina sat talking with Shannon. It was not a secret among all the friends that Shannon never thought too highly of Chaun. At times it even seemed like she despised him. It appeared to everyone that Shannon had not liked Chaun even in high school. Most thought she had misjudged Chaun's carefree and goofy spirit for immaturity. Kat continued talking, "I don't know Shannon. He has just seemed so distant lately. It's not like him. He hardly talks anymore, he just stays quiet, even on the way up here. He said maybe five words to me the entire drive up from Indianapolis."

"You know my opinion on it. Honestly, I think he's an idiot and that you could do better."

"I know how you feel and I can understand it. I love him and want to stay with him. I probably haven't been the easiest to live with since I've been pregnant and the hormones have gone crazy. I'll have spurts where I go from crying to screaming within a few minutes of each other. Give him a chance; he's not all that bad once you get to know him."

Shannon looked down, deep in thought. She looked up to where Chaun was talking with Jake. "What do you see in him?"

"Honestly, with how boyish he acts at times you wouldn't think it but, he is very intelligent. He's actually one of the smartest people I know."

"Hmmm... never would have guessed it. He always acts so dumb."

"I know. Someone meeting him for just a couple minutes wouldn't be able to guess it. It's when you get him when he's not joking or listen closely while he's joking that you can really tell."

Shannon looked at Chaun once again, raised her brow in astonishment. "I know Jake calls him the "Court Jester" of all his parties. Guess it would be kind of hard to be a jester without wits."

"I just wish he would talk more. I'm getting so sick of his quietness. It's driving me up the wall."

"Talk to him then. Convince him to tell you what's been bugging him. You aren't going to get this settled until you two talk things out."

"That's true. I'll see if I can get him to talk on the way home. Who knows, maybe we can make up if we argue on the way home."

Shannon acted like she was gagging and about ready to vomit. "That's disgusting. It's bad enough I have to see him when he has his shirt off around the pool in the summer, let alone think of him naked." Kat laughed.

"Well I better go see if he's ready to go. I know it's a long drive home and I've been decently tired lately."

Kat got up and walked over to where Chaun was talking with a few people. "Chaun, I'm ready to go. Get my coat and go start the car." Chaun looked and nodded at her for a second and started to finish his conversation. "Did you hear me? Go get my coat and start the car."

Chaun's facial expression changed and he got more of an angry distant look on his face. "If you guys will excuse me, she's ready to leave. Have a safe drive home."

One of the guys talking to Chaun said, "You too, and congrats on the baby."

Chaun gave a slight smile and he and Kat said simultaneously, "Thank you." Chaun walked to the other room, grabbed her coat, walked out, and handed it to her. She said, "Thank you." He didn't say a word as he walked out the door and started the car. Chaun returned a few minutes later. Ten minutes later he and Kat were saying goodbye to Jake and Shannon.

Jake said, "You guys drive careful and call us when you get home to let us know you made it safely."

Chaun said, "Will do. Don't have too much fun once we're gone."

Shannon gave Kat a hug and looked at Chaun, "You treat her well."

Chaun got a depressed look on his face, "I always do." *I can't believe this. Kat treats me like crap and she tells me to treat her well.* They walked out the door and Chaun opened the passenger door to their 91 Pontiac Sunbird. After Kat was safely in, he closed the door. He slowly walked around, got in the car, and backed out of the driveway.

#

The drive to the highway, after backing out of Jake's drive, took only ten minutes. It wasn't until they were driving Southbound on highway 31 that Katrina got angry enough to speak. With as little tact as possible she said, "Why the hell aren't you talking to anyone?" Chaun remained silent. "Hello? Are you deaf, or just ignoring me?"

"I'm not deaf. I just don't feel like talking right now."

"You could have fooled me. With as little as you've spoken lately someone would think you had gone deaf."

As Chaun and Katrina began to yell at each other, a blue Ford explorer pulled ahead into their blind spot in the passing lane. The Semi-truck in front of them kept at the same rate of speed. Chaun began to get more and more agitated with Kat. How could I have

8

been so blind and married someone so hateful. "Look I know your hormones have been going crazy lately, but that's no excuse to keep treating me like shit."

"I do not treat you like shit, and how dare you bring the pregnancy into this. I swear Chaun you are such a moron. You'll use any excuse available to blame everyone else."

"I do not blame everyone else."

"Yes, you do. It never fails. Whenever things start to get tough you go and blame someone else for your problems."

"I do not blame everyone else when things get tough. You want to know the reason I've been quiet and introverted lately? It's because I've been nervous as hell about the new exhibit at work. But you wouldn't know about that, because you don't shut your mouth long enough to actually listen to anyone else."

Katrina sat with her mouth open in shock. Chaun had never spoken back to her the way he had at that moment. She was furious. Her face grew red. Chaun knew what was getting ready to happen. The rant seemed to ring in his ears before her mouth started forming the words.

"How dare you talk to me like that, I'm a woman and deserve to be treated with the utmost respect. You are a worthless piece of shit. I'm eight months pregnant with our child. My hormones are going crazy and I have always treated you with respect and love. And all this time you have remained quiet and acted like a total recluse."

"You've treated me with nothing but respect and love? What reality have you been living in? Very rarely have you treated me with respect and anything close to love. You are spiteful and very hateful. I don't even know why I married you. You have made my life a living hell. I'm done. As soon as I can I'm going to file for divorce. You are mostly the reason I've remained quiet for so long. Every time I would open my mouth you would have some sort of hateful retort. I'm done with being your victim. Find someone else to treat like dirt."

It felt like everything was moving in slow motion. He saw the hurt in her eyes and the tears form at their corners. He turned to look out the windshield at the road and saw the semi slam on its brakes. Kat screamed and held onto the dashboard and door handle. He swerved onto the shoulder to miss the semi.

Chaun saw another vehicle that was stranded on the side of the road. He had already been hitting the brake as he veered onto the shoulder. He realized he wasn't slowing down enough and then realized the distance was too short to stop completely. The last thing he remembered was the car slamming into the back of the stranded vehicle and a nauseatingly painful feeling in both of his legs. Kat's screams stopped the instant of the impact.

Chapter 2

Chaun noticed the smell of a hospital and the incessant beep of a heart monitor before attempting to open his eyes. It took a long time to get his eyes open enough to see clearly. For some reason they were extremely sensitive to light and had to be opened gradually to keep the light from hurting them. Within about a half an hour he finally was able to open them to where things started to become clear.

He was lying in a hospital bed. The beeping he had heard was coming from his heart and blood pressure monitor. His nurse's name was Denise. His Dr.'s name was Smith. The table next to the hospital bed was loaded with cards that said, "Get well soon". His mind frantically rattled off question after question: What had happened after he had blacked out; How was Katrina and the baby; How long had he been asleep.

He looked down towards the bed controls and hit the button to sit up more than what he had been. He had no idea how long he had been asleep. A woman walked in to check his vitals and let out a scream and jumped when she saw Chaun sitting up with his eyes open. Her eyes, Chaun noticed, were a pale blue. How long have I been out? She is hyperventilating and so shocked at the sight of seeing me awake. She had dark brown hair and was close to, or around, 5' 6" tall.

Once she had composed herself after a couple seconds, she said, "I'm so sorry. You just startled me. My name is Denise, and I'm your nurse for today. You've been out a while. After seeing you unresponsive for so long, it just startled me." Chaun opened his mouth to speak. His mouth and throat felt as dry as Death Valley. He was not able to speak. Denise held up her hand with her index finger extended. She turned, left the room, and returned moments later with a cup of ice. She handed the cup to Chaun.

He nodded his thanks, tipped the cup towards his mouth, and began chewing a piece of ice. After he had eaten five pieces of ice, he attempted speaking once again. His voice sounded gravelly. Denise placed her hand on the bed rail. "Whisper. You don't want to strain your vocal chords. Excuse me for a couple minutes and I will go call your parents."

Chaun said, "Call my parents? What am I, in elementary school? All I'm wanting is answers." Is it so hard to answer a confused person's questions? I don't know where I am or what happened after I blacked out during the accident." His eyes bounced all over the place to find something to focus on to regain mental stability.

"I'm sorry. Our nursing staff was advised to call your parents as soon as you were awake and not to answer any major questions. I'll be right back." She then left the room.

Chaun was at a loss for words. How serious could the situation be that his parents wouldn't let the nurses answer any questions? He felt as if an enormous weight was placed on his chest. He was having trouble breathing. Chaun laced his fingers together and looked down at them trying to focus. Unable to move his legs he lifted the blanket and noticed that, not one but, both of his legs were in casts. He was thrust into chasms of confusion dissimilar to anything he had ever experienced prior to that moment. He also knew that he needed to apologize to Kat for the argument and the way he had spoken to her that night.

Denise walked out of the room and directly to the nurse's desk. She picked the phone up and dialed Dave Hutchins' cell number. "Dave?"

"Yes."

"This is Denise from the hospital. He's awake."

"Come again?"

"Chaun's awake."

"We'll be right there. Is he asking questions?"

"Yeah. I told him that you and Michelle preferred to answer any questions he may have."

"We'll be right there. We are only about 10 minutes away."

After hanging up the phone, Denise went back to Chaun's room to take his vitals. Chaun looked at Denise. She could tell by the look on his face that he was extremely confused. His face lost all color the moment she walked in. His fingers were laced in his lap, he hung his head again, eyes looking at his, she was sure, clammy hands. She placed her hand on his shoulder as she said, "Your parents will be here shortly. I stepped out a few minutes ago so I could phone them. You will have all your questions answered soon, I promise. I'm sorry for not introducing myself earlier. I'm Denise. I will be your nurse until night shift arrives. I'll see if the Dr. will be able to remove your feeding tube before they get here so you'll be more comfortable."

Chaun's head snapped upwards, his eyes meeting hers. There was questioning in his eyes. He then noticed the feeling of something protruding from his abdomen. He placed his hand on it and felt the tube that had been inserted into his abdomen through an incision. If you need anything just hit that button." She smiled, turned, and walked out of the room.

#

A few minutes later, a man entered the room in a white coat. He was taller than average with brown hair and a tan complexion. "How are you Chaun? I'm Dr. Smith. How are you feeling?"

Chaun shrugged and began with a sigh, "Extremely confused, but from what Denise says it should be cleared up soon enough."

Dr. Smith's brow furrowed and then he got a small smile on his face. "Well let's at least get that feeding tube out so you can start trying to eat naturally. How's that sound?"

16

Chaun nodded with a lack of expression on his face. "Sounds good. To tell the truth, I am pretty hungry."

Dr. Smith walked up to Chaun's left side. "This may hurt a little when we do this, but you'll feel better afterwards." He pulled the blanket back to expose the tube protruding from Chaun's abdomen. Denise entered the room with gauze and a few supplies needed for the procedure. She walked around and stopped when she reached Chaun's right side. Dr. Smith continued. "It will be quick." He said this as he started pulling the surgical tape away from the tube.

Denise laid a cloth on Chaun's stomach. Dr. Smith began to pull and with a slight popping sound the tube was removed. Denise then placed the gauze over the opening and secured it with surgical tape. "And that's it." Dr. Smith dropped the tube in the biohazard trash can followed by his gloves after removing them. He walked over to the sink, washed his hands, and turned back to Chaun. "You doing okay?"

Chaun nodded. "Yeah, thanks Doc."

"You're welcome. We'll have to ease you back onto solid food for the first couple days." Chaun nodded again to convey his understanding. "Your parents should be here shortly." Dr. Smith then walked out of the room.

"Do you want to try and eat some jello and see how it settles?"

"Anything sounds good. I am a little hungry."

Chapter 3

Dave and Michelle stepped off of the elevator. They quickly walked around the nurse's desk and continued on to Chaun's room. They were surprised when they entered and found Chaun sitting up eating jello. Dave and Michelle's faces brightened. Chaun thought it was weird. The look he read on their faces was the look of someone that had ran into a long-lost friend. Michelle ran around to the right side of Chaun's bed and threw her arms around him in a strong embrace. Dave walked up to Chaun's left side. Dave spoke in his typical gravelly voice, "They told us you were awake."

"Yep, and they've also refused to answer any questions. I was told that you preferred to answer any questions I may have."

Dave nodded. His voice grew softer. "That's true. I thought you would prefer me to tell you everything." Dave's eyes lowered. Chaun noticed Dave's brow furrow slightly.

"What do you mean everything?"

"What's the last thing you remember?"

"The last thing I remember is arguing with Kat, feeling guilty as soon as I had seen her reaction to what I said, the semi in front of us slamming on his brakes, hitting the car and feeling a pain in my legs, and then waking up here. It couldn't have been that bad could it? How long have I been out, overnight, a day or two?"

"Two months."

"Two months?!"

"You were in a coma. We just had to wait until you woke up on your own."

Chaun froze. He stared down at the jello container in his hand. He had not thought of the possibility of the damage from the accident being so severe. He got mad. His face grew red, breathing grew more labored, and his chest and shoulders began puffing up. "I take it Kat's at home with the baby enjoying her time alone?"

Dave looked at Michelle, then the floor. He looked up at Chaun. "Kat's dead. She hit her head when the car collided with the truck. She had a lot of pressure and blood around her brain. The paramedics kept her alive until they got her here. They took her for surgery and thought they had got most of the blood. Apparently, they didn't, she died two days later due to a blood clot in her heart."

The facial color that was red moments before drained leaving his face a sickly white. He grasped for rationality. He knew his parents wouldn't lie about something this serious, but part of his mind still wondered. He hoped they were lying to him so there was still a chance he could apologize for his words that night. Within a few moments he finally accepted that his parents were being truthful. As the news sank in, Chaun's face contorted.

He was falling into a chasm. The last words he said to her and that look of anguish on her face flashed through his mind. He couldn't see her face happy again, nor take back what was said. He had no way of making amends for how he had wronged her. No matter how shitty she treated him, she didn't deserve an outburst like that.

Chaun didn't feel the container fall from his hand, nor hear the clack of the container and spoon as they bounced off his cast and to the floor. He didn't notice the red trail left behind by the spilt contents. Chaun covered his face with his hands and let that dark cover blind his tears to the outside world. All that could be heard was his screams of pain. His dad stepped forward and laid his hand on Chaun's shoulder. His mom walked to him and started rubbing his back between his shoulder blades.

Dave said in almost a whisper, as he placed his hand on Chaun's shoulder, "It'll be okay son. We are here to help you through this. It's not going to be easy, but we'll help in any way we can."

"I can never take back what I said. The last look on her face, I can't erase that from memory."

"Chaun. Look at me." Chaun looked up to find his father's face portraying pure sincerity. Dave's expression was one of genuine concern. "What are you talking about?"

"Our last moments together were spent arguing. It was probably the worst fight we've ever had in all the time we'd been together. I told her she was making my life a living hell and I was leaving her. Right after I said it and saw her reaction was when the accident happened."

Dave's voice still remained calm and concerned. "That's a demon you will have to deal with on your own. For everything else we are here."

Michelle softly touched the side of Chaun's face. "Chaun. There is a little bit of good news."

"How can there be good news?" Chaun's voice raising to a yell. His face growing red again.

"They saved the baby. She's doing decent enough. They haven't released her yet. When you're ready they are still waiting to give her a name."

"Is she healthy?" Chaun sighed and his facial expression softened.

Michelle said, "She is now. It was touch and go the first few weeks, but she's out of danger now."

Chaun sighed once again and his shoulders relaxed. "Well at least there is some good news."

"Do you want to see her?"

"Not yet. I need to wrap my mind around all of this and get composed before I hold her. You know how infants are with sensing negative emotions, let alone, me being able to face her myself."

"That's true. Let us know when you're ready and we can have her brought down."

"I will. I just hope I can work through this guilt."

As he patted Chaun on the shoulder Dave said, "I know you can son. Just like your body, healing will take time."

"Speaking of which, how much damage was done."

"The car impacted at 30mph. Both of your legs were broken and you hit your head on the steering wheel. Since your rate was slow enough the airbags didn't deploy. If you were going five mph faster, the outcome may have been totally different. The airbags would have deployed and the injuries may have just been minor compared to what you both sustained."

Chaun slowly nodded his head with a distant look in his eyes. "So fate rested on a couple miles per hour. Great, next time I'll remember to slow down just enough and purposefully impact what I should attempt to avoid. If that driver would have been paying attention, we wouldn't be having this fucking conversation and my life would be continuing as normal. Then it would have just remained a damn argument that night."

\#

Dave and Michelle sat by Chaun's side for the next few hours. He went through phases of crying and being composed. His parents were surprised he was taking everything so well. Dave thought that it was partially due to shock and having so much information dumped on him within a few minutes. After some time

24

had passed, Dave said to Michelle, "Are you getting hungry?" She gave a slight nod. Dave patted her on the knee. "We'll be back son. We're going to grab some chow."

Chaun nodded, "All right pop. As soon as I can have solid food again, I wouldn't mind a burger and fries."

Dave chuckled, "You bet. I also wanted to let you know that your nurse, Denise, is one of the staff that we've grown to trust whole heartedly."

Chaun nodded, "Her demeanor does seem personable and respectful. She wouldn't answer any of my questions. After she realized I was awake she left the room to phone you. Actually, she told me outright that you two and no one else were the ones who wanted to answer my questions."

"And that's why we trust her. Most of the other nurses would probably have tried to answer some of your questions against our wishes. We'll be back in a little bit. If you have any questions, feel free to ask Denise. I'll let her know that she's trusted enough to answer any questions of yours. Love you son. We'll be back."

Chaun nodded, "Thanks dad, I love you too. Oh, while I'm thinking about it, has Jake been by?"

"He came by over the first few days and camped out. He's actually away on vacation right now. He said he'd swing by after he got back. We'll be back in a little while. Love you son."

"Love you to Dad."

As they left and walked past the nurses' station Dave spoke with Denise, "We are going for a bite to eat. Would you be able to check on him a little more than usual? I think he's partially in shock and that everything hasn't sank in fully. He is breaking down in phases."

"I would be glad to Mr. Hutchins. I'll call you if anything comes up."

"Thanks, hun."

"Are there any more restrictions to answering any of his questions?"

"With anyone else, I'd say tread carefully, but after we've got a chance to know you over the last few months, I trust your judgment and anything you'd say. You are one of the people that have been the most hospitable with our family."

Denise smiled, "Thank you. It's always nice to hear a compliment. Enjoy your dinner."

A few minutes later Denise entered Chaun's room to check his vitals and see how he was holding up. When she walked into the room, she could tell he had been crying. "Hi Denise, I must look like a mess."

Walking around to the right side of his bed and placing her hand on his arm she said, "It's okay. I'm shocked you don't seem more distraught. I know it has to be rough."

He looked at the ceiling and shook his head, "I don't think the news has fully hit me yet. It's a lot to take in. Could you do me a favor?" He looked back at her.

She made eye contact and he read complete sincerity. "Name it hun. I will help anyway I can."

"Would you be able to let the chaplain know I would like to speak with him? I want to see if he has any advice, he could give me to help deal with the guilt."

"I would be glad to let him know you're wanting to speak with him."

"Thank you."

"You're very welcome." When she turned to leave she walked up to the dry erase board. "Wasn't this filled out when I came in?"

"I think it was."

"I don't know who keeps erasing this board. Someone has been erasing it, since you arrived."

After Denise left the room his mind wandered for some time. His parents were right, she seemed very trustworthy. The look in her eyes was completely genuine. Honesty of that magnitude was rare. Chaun hoped the Chaplain would be of some help in working things out. It bothered him that losing the person he and loved for so long did not faze him the way loss would affect someone in a similar situation.

Chapter 4

Chaun was sitting up in his bed eating more jello for breakfast when an older man walked into his room. He was medium height with grey hair. The man was late 50's or early 60's. On closer inspection Chaun saw the man was holding a book in his left hand. A bible, "You must be the Chaplain."

He smiled, "That I am, my name is Charles Bishop. I was told that you wanted to speak with me."

"Yes. I was told some news yesterday that hasn't fully hit home yet. I know part of my delayed reaction is due to shock. I was wondering if you knew of some ways that I could lessen the pain and make it easier to cope once the shock wears off."

"There are a few pieces of advice I could give…" At that moment the Chaplain's glasses magnified Charles' irises changing color. The color changed from brown to black. The room, Chaun realized, had become extremely cold. What happened next, Chaun was not prepared for. Charles started an onslaught of yelling. His voice was much higher in pitch and strained. "How could you do it Chaun?"

Chaun was in disbelief. The color drained from his face and he sat agape. "Do what?"

"You know exactly what, you piece of shit! How does it feel to know that you can't take back what you said? Seeing the pain before the crash, how many times has that flashed in your mind since the accident?"

Chaun with a frightened look in his eyes responded just above a whisper, "Who told you about the accident?" The black in Charles' eyes seemed to drain back into his pupils. He looked at Chaun with a total look of shock and confusion. He didn't say a word. He just turned on his heels and bolted from the room.

Denise heard the commotion, saw the Chaplain leave Chaun's room, and briskly walked past the nurses' station with his head down. She watched him enter the elevator. As soon as the doors were closed, she went directly to Chaun's room. When she entered, she was dumbfounded. Chaun was sitting in bed with a blank look on his face. The tracks of tears shimmered in the light. "You okay?"

Chaun's reply was monotone, "I don't know. Does the Chaplain normally seem like he needs a shrink?"

Her brow furrowed with concern and anger. "I heard it from the station. What all happened?"

"He came in, we started having a normal conversation, and then things went crazy."

Denise raised her right eyebrow, "Crazy as in just him yelling at you?"

"No, crazy as in, he stopped mid-sentence. Then his eyes changed color. After that he started yelling at me. He started placing blame on me for the accident. The room got extremely cold as well. Has someone told him about the accident?"

"Not to my knowledge. My letting him know you wanted to talk to him is the only information I gave him. I don't know how he would have known about the accident."

Denise shook her head, her face retaining confusion. "That's weird. He was going on about the accident and then right before he bolted from the room it was almost as if his pupils sucked the black color from his irises."

"That is strange. Are you going to be okay?" She placed her hand on his left hand.

"Yeah, it just caught me off-guard and started bringing up guilty feelings again."

She patted his hand and smiled at Chaun, "If you need anything you know how to get ahold of me."

Chaun nodded, "I'll keep that in mind. Are you typically allowed to sit and talk with patients after hours?" He smiled slightly.

"Not typically, but they sometimes make exceptions. I'm sure with your case they wouldn't mind."

"Thanks. It just gets kind of boring sitting here in the evening. Granted, I've last night and prior hospitalizations to form that opinion. TV can only hold your attention for so long."

Denise laughed, "That's true. Let's see how the rest of my day goes. I may be able to talk for a couple minutes before I head out."

\#

When Dave and Michelle stepped off the elevator, Denise raised her hand, "Dave." Dave and Michelle walked up to the nurses' desk. Dave stood across the desk from her.

Dave asked, "He doing okay?"

Dave could tell something was off. Her facial expression told him that things had not gone smoothly after they had left. "The Chaplain came to see him while you were gone. Chaun had asked me yesterday to see if the Chaplain would be able to come and speak with him."

As if to himself, Dave asked, "Why did he do that?"

"I don't know," her brow furrowed and she about broke down in tears, "I could hear the Chaplain yelling from out here. I went in after he left the room and Chaun had this blank, shocked look on his face with tears running down his cheeks. He said that the Chaplain had stopped mid-sentence and started yelling at him. He said it was weird. Somehow the Chaplain knew about the accident. I said nothing to him about the situation."

Denise became a little frightened by the look on Dave's face. It started turning red as his eyebrows angled downward when the bridge of his nose compressed in an expression of anger. She could tell that his breathing became heavier and deeper. Denise thought that, at any second, he would blow up at her. She winced and recoiled slightly thinking Dave's few moments of silence was him preparing to blow up at her. Instead he calmly said, "If you'll excuse

me, I think I'm going to talk to the Chaplain."

Chapter 5

When Dave entered the hospital Chapel, he was surprised to find the Chaplain sitting on the second pew from the front. If Dave had shown up on any other day, he would have found the Chapel nice for its size. It had red carpet, three to four rows of pews, and a nice-looking cross hanging above the altar with a false stained-glass window behind it. Dave was still boiling as he walked up to the man in the pew. "Are you the Chaplain?"

The Chaplain quietly turned and said, "That depends on who is asking."

"I'm Dave Hutchins, Chaun Hutchins father."

"Yes I'm the Chaplain. Charles Bishop." He held out his hand hoping Dave would shake it. He just stood looking down at it. Charles could tell that Dave was about ready to explode.

Dave's arms shot up from his sides. "What the hell were you thinking?"

Charles motioned with his hand to the pew in front of him. His voice soft and shaky. "Please sit."

Dave calmed for a second realizing the man was willing to talk things out peacefully. His arms lowered returning to his sides and his shoulders relaxed. Something didn't seem right. Why would someone be willing to talk so peacefully and keep calm after yelling at someone for no valid reason? He sat down sideways with his right arm resting on the back of the pew. "What the hell were you thinking?"

"I wasn't, all I remember is that I was in the middle of a sentence when it felt like something took over. I don't remember anything about the hospital room for the next few minutes, and then I was back in the hospital room. When I came back around Chaun was staring at me with his mouth agape. When he asked how I knew about the accident I knew something had gone on that was beyond explanation at that moment."

Dave paused attempting not to laugh after seeing the serious look on the Chaplain's face. "When you say you were no longer in the hospital room, what do you mean?"

"I mean I was seeing something else." Dave could tell that the Chaplain was completely confused. The Chaplain's face portrayed an eccentric state. The look was serious yet lost, as if he was reasoning back and forth within his mind grasping for viable answers.

"Did you see or hear anything, was it total darkness?"

Charles got quiet and looked down. He tried to find the words to describe it. "It was like… like I was dreaming. I was sitting in the passenger seat of a car. Chaun was yelling at me and being tactless. To sum it up he said I was making his life a living hell and he wanted a divorce. I felt nothing but shock and emotional pain. The next thing I remember was seeing the brake lights of a semi, swerving, and seeing another vehicle before the car collided with it. The entire time I could hear a woman screaming. As soon as the collision occurred, the screaming stopped. Then I was back in the hospital room with Chaun looking like he had just witnessed something totally unbelievable."

Dave's face slowly regained its color as the Chaplain explained everything, then it kept losing color until he was pallid. "So, no one told you about the accident before you walked into the room, or even gave you any background as to the reason of Chaun being in the hospital?"

Charles shook his head confused and exasperated. "Nothing. All I was told is that he wished to speak with me."

Dave nodded. His face had regained some of its color. He looked down at the pew he was sitting on then back up at Charles. "Chaplain, you just described the accident that killed Chaun's wife. He said some awful things to her that night out of anger. He was driving and was able to slow down enough that the airbags didn't deploy, which unfortunately caused him to be in a coma for two months and cause Kat's death."

Charles got quiet for a few moments and with an expression of total confusion said, "How is that possible?"

"I don't know Chaplain, but apparently it is very possible. God is only half of the reality in Christianity. Anyone in your line of work knows this. Granted, this is my opinion but, the other half is just as real, and that's where people have issues with accepting the other side of reality. Most Christians focus on the happy bliss of Christianity, but at the same time they walk blindly around not accepting that the Devil truly exists as well as his minions."

The Chaplain nodded his head. "Very true, God promises that the devil can only tempt us. That's where most Christians believe it ends. They believe that due to their faith that they are immune from the truth of demons existing here on earth. The Bible discusses two separate instances of possession within the book of Luke. It's, I believe, chapters four and eight. Most read that and think that God can conquer any foe. People don't look at the bold-faced reality that possessions do exist."

"They do exist, and it is possible that something took possession of your body in that room. That could be the reason you weren't mentally in that hospital room the entire time. You do work in a hospital and they are known to have a lot of paranormal activity."

Charles looked towards the floor, pursed his lips, and nodded his head in agreement. "That is a fact. Most of the paranormal investigators now find that hospitals are hotspots for paranormal activity. You surprise me Mr. Hutchins."

Dave chuckled, "I know, I'm smarter than I look."

Charles laughed. "I wouldn't put it that way. In this day and age, you don't meet too many people who expand their horizons enough to come up with valid arguments like you just made. Most people today are ignorant regarding certain issues. They are happy with living their lives the same day in and day out." The longer they talked the more Dave noticed that Charles was the type of person that used their hands to emphasize certain words while he spoke.

"That is true. I've always believed that knowledge is power. Ignorance doesn't supply happiness, only more difficult trials." Dave extended his hand to Charles. Charles reached out accepting Dave's handshake. "If you or your family need anything while Chaun's here feel free to stop by or call."

"We'll keep it in mind. Nice talking with you Chaplain." Dave stood with the opposite body language from what he portrayed entering the Chapel. His shoulders, arms, and hands were relaxed. His facial color and vocal tones were normal.

"Likewise, Mr. Hutchins, if Chaun is willing to talk again I can try stopping by again sometime in the near future. I'd like to apologize for my behavior, even though I wasn't mentally present."

"I'm sure he would be more than willing to speak with you again." Maybe this time you will get to finish your conversation." Dave smiled as Charles nodded his head. Dave turned and pushed open the Chapel doors, and left to head back to Chaun's room.

Chapter 6

A few days later, Dave and Michelle were sitting in the room with Chaun. The conversation, to that point, consisted of typical, everyday context. To their surprise Chaun said, "How is the baby?"

Dave said, "She's good. The Dr. said she might be able to leave soon."

Chaun smiled and nodded his head. "That's good. Can I see her?"

Dave smiled ear to ear. Chaun rarely saw Dave show so much emotion. He was half expecting Dave to start jumping up and down. "I'll go right up and see if they can bring her down."

"Thanks dad." Dave nodded his head in response. Michelle looked as if she were going to start crying. Chaun started laughing lightly.

Michelle's face went from watery eyes to furrowed brow. "Don't you dare laugh at your mother when she's crying Chaun Hutchins. That's a mean thing to do when someone is trying to show genuine emotion."

Chaun's body started shaking from trying to stifle his ever-increasing laughter. "I can't help it."

"Yes, you can. Don't lie to your mother, that's mean." She started, again, shaking her finger at Chaun as she was talking. This made Chaun start laughing out loud. "Stop it. Stop it right now." Michelle began to break and began laughing along with Chaun.

As Chaun and Michelle's laughter began to subside he said, "Why were you crying anyways?"

Michelle sat down on the bed facing Chaun. She placed her hand on his. "Think about it Chaun. It's the first time you are going to see something that is part of you. Aren't you nervous at all?"

"I'm petrified. What if I'm a failure as a father?" Chaun's brow furrowed and his eyes portrayed absolute fear.

"Wait until you hold her, then I will give you the answer to that question." She patted his hand and Chaun could tell she was holding back tears. Yet, this time, he didn't laugh.

#

Dave returned 15 minutes later, followed by a nurse pushing a hospital baby bed. Chaun noticed how fast his heart was beating. He also noticed his palms were sweaty. Chaun knew he would be nervous, just not to this extreme. The nurse placed his daughter in his arms. As soon as he saw her with her beautiful brown hair and blue eyes, he was pummeled by a tidal wave of emotion. He had not thought of how strongly he would be touched by this moment.

Michelle asked, "Do you love her?"

"More than anything mom."

"Chaun," Chaun looked up to meet Michelle's gaze, "remember that feeling, and you will not fail her." A tear dropped from Chaun's eye and ran down his cheek. "Now you understand why I was crying earlier. I knew it was going to be an amazing and memorable moment for you both."

Chaun nodded and looked back at his daughter, "I understand now mom. I'm sorry I laughed at you."

"Do you have a name for her yet?"

"Kat wanted to name her Samantha Noel. I think that would be a gift from her mother." Chaun looked up at his parents with total sincerity. "I need to ask you if you would do something for me."

Dave answered, "All you have to do is ask son."

"If she is released before I am, would you two be willing to take her home and care for her? At least until I can heal enough to be released from the hospital."

"We would be glad to. Actually, your dad has already converted the room next to your old room into a nursery just in case."

"Thank you so much."

Chapter 7

Denise walked into Chaun's hospital room. Chaun gave a slight smile. She said, "My shift just ended. I can only stay about ten minutes. That is all the time my supervisors would allow."

"Ten minutes is better than no time at all."

"That's true."

"Please, have a seat." Chaun motioned with his hand to the chair next to the hospital bed.

Denise sat down in the chair. With her eyes closed and she let out a sigh. Chaun thought she must have had a long day. When her eyes opened she was smiling and focused on nothing but Chaun. "So, how are you holding up with everything?"

Chaun looked down trying to find the right words. "Better than I should be. Granted, I've had so much going on since I woke up. More than likely, it will really hit once I get home."

Chaun could tell that she was still listening. Her eyes told him everything he needed to know. In those eyes were genuine caring and concern. He couldn't believe someone could feel so much concern for another in such a short time. She then asked, "Are you afraid?"

"Am I afraid of when it fully sinks in?" Denise nodded. "I'm terrified. I have never had something to this extreme happen in my life until now."

"I honestly think you'll get through it. To me you seem like a strong-willed person."

"Only to a point, my snapping at Kat the night of the accident was one of the few times I defended myself, in all the years we had been together."

Denise sat agape. "Was your marriage that bad?"

"It had its moments. Most of the harshness came from Katrina. I don't usually talk poorly about someone who has passed," Chaun looked at his hands folded and resting on his lap. His face was blank as he said, "but with Kat it's the truth."

Denise's brow lowered as her eyes squinted in curiosity. "What was she like?"

"She had to have her way all of the time." Chaun looked up at Denise and as he continued speaking, she began to sense how much pain Katrina had caused Chaun. "Kat was a control freak. Our home had very little on the walls. Most of the color in the apartment was black and white. Everything in the house had its place. She hardly asked me for anything. She always would demand things of me instead. That was part of the reason I had blown up at her that night."

She lowered her head briefly. "I'm sorry you had to go through that. I've had my share of bad relationships in the past. They are never easy."

"I know, eventually, I will have to move on. To be honest, and don't take this the wrong way but, I hope she has traits similar to yours. You seem so caring, open, and personable. It would be a nice change from living around Kat for so long."

A tear fell from Denise's eye, "For your sake, and your daughter, I hope so. I don't want this to sound bad, but I think you would be happier with someone with those qualities."

"I think you're right. My relationship with Kat was pretty miserable." Chaun paused and looked down once again. "Don't get me wrong. I love her, and always will, but I need to stay strong. Sam needs me to be a beacon of strength. Granted, I know she's only an infant, but if memory serves me correctly, infants can sense the feelings of those around them." He looked at Denise. "I'm sorry. Here I am rambling on about myself and my issues. I really do want to learn more about you. Where are you from originally?"

"I am actually from Colorado. I moved here a few years ago."

Chaun sat back, resting his head on his pillow and looking at the ceiling said, "Man, I miss the Rockies."

"You lived in Colorado?"

Chaun nodded his head and turned to Denise, head still on the pillow, "Yeah. Dad was stationed at Ft. Carson for a few years. It's a gorgeous area. I miss the mountains the most though." His eyes grew distant yet focused as he visually pictured mental images from memory. "It was so peaceful to sit in the mountains and look at the city thousands of feet below."

A man then entered the room. Chaun almost started laughing. He was wearing a suit and at the most had to be about five feet tall. He had short blonde hair and, from what Chaun could tell at a distance, blue eyes. Chaun felt bad for his reaction. The man had simply caught him off guard. The man almost looked like a kid dressed up for church. "Chaun Hutchins?" Chaun nodded. "I'm

Chris Hastings. I'm handling the litigation of the trucking company on your behalf."

Denise stood up. "I better go. My ten minutes are just about up. I'm working again tomorrow. I'll see you then."

Chaun smiled and nodded. "Thank you for the visit. I hope it won't be the only one. Have a good one, and drive safe."

"I will. You be sure to get some rest." She left the room.

Chaun's right eye squinted as he looked back at Chris and said, "I don't remember signing any litigation paperwork against the trucking company."

"You didn't. Your parents called my office to get everything rolling. At minimum they thought it would help with Dr. bills and income supplement while you're recovering and getting your life back together."

"I'm fine with anything you think is fair. I know any amount will be helpful. How much are you asking for?"

"Five million."

Chaun sat staring at Chris. His eyes were wide and his breathing grew labored. Chris watched as Chaun's experienced a sensory overload. Chaun exclaimed a second later, "Five million?! I

49

don't need that much, but if that's what you're going for then I'm cool with it. I'm pretty sure after Sam and I being in the hospital for so long, the bills have to be piling up. Just keep me posted on what's going on with the litigation."

"You will know the day of. I am going to need you to show up in court."

Chaun gave a slight nod of his head. "As long as I'm out of the hospital, I'll be able to make it to the proceedings. Do I need to sign the paperwork now or on the court date?"

"You'll have to sign on the court date. I'll keep you posted though. Do you mind if I sit?"

Chaun motioned to the chair. "No, not at all."

Chris walked over and sat down with an exhausted look on his face. "Thanks, it's been a long day. Do you mind answering some questions?"

Chaun shook his head. "Not at all. What do you need to know?"

Chris looked at Chaun with total concentration. "How did it happen that night? I know what the police reports say from witnesses and the driver's statement, but I want to know what happened from your perspective. If you are still needing some time emotionally to cope with everything, we can wait."

Chaun exhaled and looked down in his lap. He interlaced his fingers. "I'm okay with talking about it. How detailed are you wanting the description?"

Chris chuckled, "You don't need to draw any pictures or anything, but as detailed an account as you can give."

Chaun smirked, nodded, and then looked back at his hands lying in his lap. "We were on our way home from a party. I did not drink that night."

Looking at his notebook Chris said, "The Drs. did toxicology on you when you arrived. They said that you had no alcohol in your system. Go on."

Chaun gave a slight nod in response. "Tension had been building between us for some time. I lost my cool and we started arguing. I had been quiet for a couple months prior to the accident."

"Were you thinking of leaving her or anything of that nature?"

Chaun shook his head. His brow slightly furrowed as he said, "No, I would have never left her, especially with her being pregnant.

The argument escalated and I pretty much told her she was making my life a living hell and I wanted a divorce. I didn't mean it. I was just sticking up for myself for the first time in years."

Chris' right eyebrow raised. "Why did you feel the need to stick up for yourself?"

"She was constantly demanding and controlling. I was never able to do anything I wanted to do without being ridiculed." Chris nodded his head. "As soon as I told her that I looked up to see the brake lights of the semi light up. I swerved to miss the truck and didn't have enough distance to stop before hitting the stranded vehicle."

"What details do you remember about the vehicle? The one on the shoulder. Do you remember if the hazard lights were on?"

Chaun made eye contact with Chris. "I remember it very well. It's the last thing I remember seeing from that night. The hazard lights were not flashing."

Chris knew Chaun's statement was factual and added the information to his notepad. "Were you the typical two seconds behind the semi when it hit its brakes?"

Chaun nodded and maintained eye contact with Chris. His voice rose enough to let Chris know he was serious without being defensive. "Yes. I am a very defensive driver. Most comment that I drive like an old lady. There's another thing, the semi didn't just lightly hit its brakes. The tires were squalling."

Chris wrote down the last bit of information and placed the items in his briefcase. "Thank you so much, that should be all I need for now. Your story matches up closer to that of the witnesses than the driver." Chris stood up and reached out his hand to shake Chaun's. "Again, thank you for your time. I am truly sorry for your loss."

Chaun accepted Chris' handshake. "Thank you, Mr. Hastings. If there is any more information you need feel free to come by or call."

"I will, until we talk again, rest and get well. Like I said I will keep you informed." As Chris turned and left the room Chaun's mind began to wander. He thought of everything being paid off and Samantha being able to go through college. In some ways he would give it all back and say forget the entire court issue, if he could just know that Kat was still alive and was able to spend time with their

daughter.

Chapter 8

Dave and Michelle walked into Chaun's room. Something
was different. They were grinning ear to ear. Chaun quizzically
looked at them both. "Something's up. What is it?"

Michelle could not contain herself. "We just came from
upstairs. Sam's Dr. is going to come down shortly and speak with
you. They are going to need you to sign some papers." She walked
up to the right side of Chaun's bed, sat down, and placed her hand on
his. "They've decided that she is ready to go home."

Chaun smiled, "That's great! Hopefully I'll be leaving soon
as well."

The Dr. walked into the room sooner than expected. She
looked young for her age. Chaun would have guessed her in her late
20's. In reality she was in her early 40's. By her physique Chaun
guessed her a runner. "Mr. Hutchins?"

"Yes."

The Doctor approached Chaun on his left side. Her hand
extended. Chaun accepted the handshake. She smiled as she said,
"Hi, I'm Dr. Spalding. I'm Samantha's Dr."

"Yes ma'am."

As she continued her hands began to move. The movements added personality and enthusiasm to what she was saying. "I wanted to come down and speak with you about Sam. She has made tremendous improvement over the past month. I believe that she is ready to go home. Part of the reason we have kept her here this long is due to needing your signature to have her leave the hospital, not to mention having a place for her to go. Your parents have notified me that you have asked them to watch over her until your release. Is this correct?"

"Yes, ma'am, it is. I asked them the first day I held her if they would take care of her if she were to be released before me." Chaun nodded towards Dave and Michelle. "They said they would be more than happy to. They already have the nursery prepared."

"In that case, I will need your signature on the release paperwork. There shouldn't be any restrictions for her care. She is as healthy as a normal baby." She handed Chaun a clipboard with the paperwork needing signed. Chaun took it, signed it after scanning it over, and handed it back to her. Dr. Spalding turned to Dave and Michelle. "Mr. and Mrs. Hutchins, if you'd want to come back upstairs, we can get her personal things and release her into your care." Dave and Michelle both followed the Dr. out of the room. Knowing that Sam was being released gave Chaun hope that he would also be released in the near future.

A little while later, Michelle returned to the room holding Sam. Chaun asked, "Dad loading up her stuff in the car?"

Michelle looked up at Chaun and nodded. "Yeah, he should be back up in a few minutes. You wanting to hold her."

Chaun smiled, "Of course I want to hold her. Why wouldn't I?" Michelle walked over and handed Sam to Chaun. "How soon are you guys heading out?"

"Shortly. It is an hour drive home, and with her being so little, it will probably wear her out."

Chaun raised his brow in agreement and nodded. "That is true. Be sure you guys call me when you get there and let me know you made it."

"We will. Don't worry, she's in good hands."

"I know she is." Dave walked into the room. "She couldn't have had that much stuff?"

Dave sighed and looked at Chaun with a smirk. He pointed at Michelle, "You have no idea." Michelle playfully slapped Dave on the shoulder.

Michelle said, "Oh stop it Dave." All three of them laughed. She turned and looked back at Chaun. "If you are okay with it, I think we will go ahead and start heading that way. Like I said it is going to be a long drive, especially for the little one."

Chaun handed Sam back to Michelle who then put her in her car seat. "That's fine. Like I said though, just call and let me know you guys made it safely."

Dave said, "We will. You take it easy. The more you rest the sooner you will be able to come home. We have kept your room how it's always been. The nursery is set up where my old office used to be, right next door to your old room."

Chaun nodded. "That's cool. Hopefully I'll be able to be back in it sooner than later."

"I hope so son." As they turned to leave Dave said, "Love you son."

"Love you guys too, drive safe."

Michelle said, "We will. We'll call you when we get home."

Dave and Michelle walked out of the room with Sam.

#

On the drive home, Dave drove and Michelle sat in the back of their Black Lincoln Navigator with Sam. They would have loved to say the trip was uneventful, but unfortunately that was not the case. They had just left the outskirts of Ft. Wayne heading south. Sam was sleeping. Dave and Michelle were talking about Chaun. Michelle began to shiver. She began to rub her arms to try and regain some warmth. "Do you have the air conditioning on?"

Dave looked at the dashboard. He shook his head and looked back at Michelle in the rearview mirror. "No, it's off and all the windows are up. It does feel quite a bit colder in here though. How's Sam?" Michelle looked down at Sam to check on her. She let out a scream as Sam's eyes snapped open to reveal not her usual blue eyes but pitch black. Sam's head turned to where the eyes were focused directly at Michelle. Dave looked at Michelle in the rearview mirror. "Michelle, what's wrong?" Michelle didn't move. She was terrified. She just sat there with her hands shaking and peering into those black eyes. The color had drained from her face.

What Dave and Michelle heard next, almost made Dave jump out of his skin. Sam began to speak in a drawn-out high-pitched voice. "Your son's an ass hole. You know that don't you?" Dave kept switching his glance from the road to Michelle in the mirror. He knew it wasn't Michelle talking due to her mouth not moving.

With quivering voice, Michelle answered back, "Who are you?"

The voice speaking through Sam said, "Who I am is not important. This is your warning. Chaun's life will be a living hell."

Michelle sat with her mouth hanging open and face twisted between terror and pain. "How can you say that?"

Sam's eyebrows furrowed enhancing the menacing black orbs, "I will be the cause of his ruined life. He cannot escape me, no matter what he does." Michelle watched Sam's irises fade to their normal blue color. The car had warmed back up from how cold it had been the previous few moments.

She looked at Dave's eyes in the rearview mirror. He returned her gaze. Dave asked, "Is it gone?"

"Yes." Michelle's voice still sounded weak. She cowered against the car door and didn't look at Sam. Nothing was said the remainder of the drive home.

Chapter 9

Chaun sat in his bed, looking at the cast that ran the full length of his leg. Most of the reason he was still here was due to that leg. His other leg had broken below the knee. The X-ray techs had just left his room after taking x-rays of his leg. His parents had been home with Sam a couple days now. They had called the day they had taken her home and said that she was doing fine. They had also said that she had done fine on the ride home.

About 20 minutes later, Dr. Smith walked through the door into Chaun's room. "How are you this morning Chaun?"

"I'm good."

"That's good to hear. Your x-rays came back, and your leg is healed. I'm going to have someone take you down and get it removed. It healed sooner than expected. Since you were in the coma, motionless for two months, and that it was a clean break all helped in the healing process. We can supply you a boot for your other leg, but I don't want you on your feet other than for a few seconds or minutes at a time. It will take a little while to build your strength back up in the leg. You will probably be in a wheelchair for the next week or two."

Chaun made eye contact with the Doctor. "How soon before I get to go home?"

"We want to make sure you can walk well enough and that nothing happens to break the leg again or hurt any of the muscles or connective tissue. You have been off of it and not used those muscles for some time."

Chaun nodded his head. "Thank you, Dr."

"You're very welcome."

A few hours later, Chaun was back in his hospital bed. The cast removal went smoothly. They said his leg looked fine. Chaun was unsure of how much longer it would be until he could go home. It was all up the Dr. Smith. Chaun was tired of sitting in a damn hospital bed. He wished he could just get up and walk around. The leg had been difficult to move since the cast was removed. They said it would take some time to get it moving again. He kept trying to move it little by little.

Dr. Smith walked into the room followed by Denise. "How does your leg feel?"

Chaun rubbed his leg, smiled, and looked at Dr. Smith. "It feels good, doesn't itch as much as what it did, still hard to move though."

Dr. Smith started lifting and prodding his leg checking the usual stuff: pain, circulation, color. He gave a slight laugh. "Of course, it's going to be hard to move. It's been lying in the same position for over two months." Chaun gave a slight laugh and grin. "Does this hurt?" He began to flex Chaun's leg holding under Chaun's knee and pushing on the top of the ankle.

"Nope, just sore."

"That's good." Dr. Smith patted Chaun's leg below the knee. "Your leg muscles have atrophied, but that is due to not being used for the last couple months." He picked up Chaun's chart and updated his notes as he continued speaking. "We'll keep you a few more days to see how things go with getting that leg moving and to make sure nothing will get injured the more you use it."

"Thanks Doc." Chaun paused, then asked with a hopeful tone, "Is there any possibility of me going down to the cafeteria to get my lunch instead of them bringing it to the room. I'd like to see something outside of this room for a bit."

The Dr. thought for a moment. "I don't see any harm in it. Of course, you won't be able to go on your own. I'll see if one of the nursing staff would be able to take you. Sound good?"

He smiled and nodded, "That sounds great. Thank you, Dr. Smith."

"You're very welcome." Chaun beamed.

#

Denise pushed a wheel chair into the room a short time later. She pushed it right up to Chaun's bed. "You ready? I took my break so we won't be as rushed to get back up to the floor. I've got an hour."

"Awesome." He began moving to the edge of his bed. As he slowly tried to stand Denise helped support his weight. Chaun smiled. "You didn't have to."

Denise smiled, "It's okay. It will be a decent change of lunch conversation than my normal." Denise placed her hands on Chaun's arm to help him if needed. He noticed the softness of her hands. Her lotion or perfume was honeydew melon and cucumber. Once he was in the wheelchair, Denise backed it up and pushed him out into the hallway.

"Depending on how crowded the floor is, my breaks are usually between thirty minutes to an hour. And today is your lucky day because there are a lot of empty beds."

As Denise started pushing the wheelchair down the hallway towards the elevator Chaun gave a slight laugh. "That's good to know."

The walls outside of his room were painted a light green on top and midnight blue below the wooden rail. The carpet was cobalt blue with golden bordering. When they reached the elevators, Denise pushed the down button. They both waited in silence for the elevator to arrive with its typical ding followed by sliding doors. After the person arriving on the floor did the typical scurry out of the doors, Denise pushed Chaun into the elevator and pushed the button for the basement.

Chaun's brow, though unseen by Denise, rose slightly. "I didn't get a chance to ask you the other night. How long have you been a nurse?"

"I've been a nurse for about five years. Started out in Colorado, got into a bad relationship," she paused, took a deep breath, then let out a long sigh, "and moved out here to get away from him."

Chaun's brow furrowed, "I'm sorry you had to experience such a horrid relationship."

Denise looked like it did not bother her. She smiled halfheartedly still trying to suppress her painful past. "It's not your fault. Some men are just ass holes and you can't change that. I've learned from it and know not to stay with a guy that does not appreciate me."

"You seem really strong willed. That's a good quality to have, I admire you for it." Chaun tilted his head back to look into Denise's eyes. His comment was genuine. He chided himself mentally for not having Denise's strength earlier in his relationship with Katrina.

Denise blushed slightly. "Thank you." The bell sounded and she pushed the wheelchair out of the elevator. She walked down towards the cafeteria. The entire way Chaun was just enjoying not being in the hospital room like he had since waking up. He was surprised at how much he was just enjoying the feeling of movement. They arrived in the cafeteria to find that it was almost empty. The seating area was quite large. It consisted of both tables and booths. It looked to easily seat 250 to 300 people. There were plants placed around the room.

Denise fixed herself a salad with ranch dressing from the salad bar. Chaun ordered a grilled cheese and tomato soup. They both paid for their meals. Denise pushed Chaun to a table and sat down opposite him. A mother and little girl sat nearby. Chaun watched them and got very quiet. His thoughts drifted to what might have been, if they had done one thing differently that night. Even a change of a few seconds either way would have saved Kat's life. Denise noticed him watching the mother and daughter. She saw the distant look of painful curiosity. "You okay?"

Chaun blinked. He shook his head slightly as if attempting to clear the thoughts from his head. "Hmm? Yeah, just wondering what things would be like if we had left early or waited for even a few seconds longer that night."

The little girl had to be no older than eight with long brown hair. Her mom had told her not to blow bubbles in her milk. She turned and looked at Chaun, and continued to blow bubbles in her milk where she thought her mother wouldn't notice.

The mother looked up at her daughter after taking a bite of food. Her brow furrowed slightly at the sight of her daughter's refusal to listen. She reached out and pulled at the fabric of the girl's sleeve. "Laura Ann turn around, quit blowing bubbles in your milk, and eat your food. Leave that poor man alone."

Chaun gave a slight smile. "She's quite alright ma'am."

The woman's brow leveled. She rested back into her seat. "You sure? You looked agitated or upset."

"I was, but not because she was looking at me. She made me reflect on what might have been."

She looked at Denise and then back at Chaun. "Do you two have any children?"

Denise blushed and Chaun joined her in a laugh. "No ma'am. This is one of my nurses. My daughter is with my parents."

The mother's eyes widened. Her tone was apologetic as she said, "Oh, is your wife there with her?"

Chaun's eyes looked downwards at the comment. His brow furrowed as he looked up. "No, she passed away a couple months ago." The mother gasped and raised her hand to her mouth. "We had been in a car accident and the Drs. weren't able to save her. They were able to save my daughter though. I just woke up two weeks ago after being in a coma."

The Mother's hand moved from her mouth to her chest, "I'm sorry I didn't know."

The mother was surprised to find that Chaun's face portrayed nothing but genuine understanding and absolutely no offense had been taken. "It's quite alright ma'am. You had no way of knowing. Your daughter just got me thinking of what things could have been like between my wife and Samantha if she had lived."

The mother nodded. "So that's why you looked hurt or agitated? I wish things could have worked out that way. Sorry I didn't introduce myself earlier. I'm Sophia and this is Laura Ann."

Chaun nodded. "Nice to meet you Sophia, I'm Chaun and this is Denise. Hopefully I'll be able to go home soon so I can spend time with Samantha." His shoulders relaxed, he looked down, then raised his head smiling. "Any advice for a new parent?"

Sophia's tone softened. She looked at Chaun with an intensity that portrayed total caring and love that only mothers of a selfless nature can comprehend. "Mostly just be patient with them. I know it seems overwhelming at times, but it's a wonderful experience if you can just remain patient during the chaotic times." She laughed. "Make sure you tell her you love her and show it by your actions that she is loved. Make her the center of your attention when she needs it. Cherish the time you have. It goes by fast."

Chaun smiled and looked at Laura Ann who returned the gesture complete with empty spaces of shadow amid white. "Thank you, I will keep it in mind."

"You're welcome." She looked at Laura Ann. "You ready to go sweetie. We've got to get home so we can let the dog out." Laura Ann nodded her head while still drinking her milk. They got up and started walking out of the cafeteria. Sophia and Laura Ann stopped in front of the table at which Chaun and Denise were sitting. She shook hands with both of them. "It was nice meeting the both of you. I hope everything works out for you and Samantha."

Chaun reached out to shake Laura Ann's hand smiling. She accepted. "Thank you, it was nice meeting you two as well. Have a good day."

"You too." The two then walked out of the cafeteria passing the table at which they had been sitting. Laura Ann turned back once and waved.

After Sophia and Laura Ann left, Denise looked at Chaun. She could tell he was on the verge of tears. "You all right?"

He nodded as a tear fell. He wiped it away. "Yeah, just still mulling over what might have been if I had made even one decision differently that night, and how different things might be today."

"I understand. Chaun, look at me." Chaun looked up into Denise's eyes. Her eyes were penetrating and stern, yet her brow was raised. Her tone was demanding and caring. "You need to quit beating yourself up over this. You had no way of knowing what was going to happen, let alone what minor differences would have caused things to change. No matter what we face in life, trials have to be taken as they come. We can never change the past, but only better ourselves for the future."

Chaun nodded in agreement. "You're right. I just have to deal with what is and not what could have been."

The rest of their conversation consisted of small talk. They finished eating and returned to the hospital floor where Chaun's room was located.

Chapter 10

Chaun didn't bother looking up when a familiar voice spoke. "Don't tell me you're still in this damn hospital." Jake was standing just inside the door to Chaun's hospital room. Chaun knew by the tone of his voice that he had his typical smirk plastered across his face.

Chaun looked up. There it was, that smirk. Chaun grinned stretched between his ears. "I see you finally stopped by for a visit." Chaun started laughing. Jake walked over and, to Chaun's surprise, gave Chaun a hug. "How the hell have you been?"

Chaun nodded his head. He motioned to the chair next to his bed. Jake sat. "I've been okay. How are you holding up?"

"They just took my full leg cast off the other day. They said I will probably be able to go home in a couple of days to a week, pending I don't reinjure my leg."

Jake smiled, "That's good." His smile faded to a sullen frown. "I'm sorry about Kat. It's lousy, how things worked out."

Chaun lowered his eyes and head, then looked back up at Jake. "I know it is. If one thing had delayed us, or gone differently that night, she may still be here. Luckily the baby is healthy and doing well. How's Shannon doing since everything happened? I know she hasn't thought much of me over the years. You know I'm not as heartless as she thinks."

Jake's eyebrows raised as he sat back in the chair. "She's holding up okay. Of course, being Shannon, she blames you for Kat's death."

"Of course, she does." Chaun looked at the boards on the wall in front of him. "Did you make it to the funeral?"

Jake looked down at his hand as he was fretting with a scratch on the armrest of the chair. "Yeah, it was a good service. You seem like you're handling the situation pretty well."

Chaun shrugged his shoulders and turned to look at Jake once again. "Not much else to do when you're sitting in a hospital bed and can't move. I've had a lot of time to think. The guilt has been overwhelming at times, but it's something I am going to have to learn to cope with. There's not much I can do to make amends."

Jake gave Chaun a questioning look, "What are you talking about?"

Chaun sighed as he lowered his gaze to the floor between them. His expression darkened. "We were fighting when the accident happened. You know how I hardly ever stuck up for myself during the relationship?" Jake nodded. "Well I let her have it that night. I didn't hit her, but the look on her face the seconds before the accident happened..." He looked back at Jake. His brow raised. "I may as well have. I was ruthless in my choice of words that night." His right hand balled into a fist and he enclosed it with his left. "Hell, I wasn't even thinking of what I was saying."

Jake's hand stopped messing with the chair arm. He look up and sat forward slightly. "What did you say to her?"

Chaun's eyes glazed over with a distant stare. "To sum it up I told her she was making my life a living hell, and that I was going to file for divorce. I was so sick of the mistreatment and feeling like I was not important to her."

Jake's voice rose and sounded almost defensive. "I know she never treated you well, but no one would deserve that. She was eight months pregnant with your baby." Jake's face started to turn red. "So your last memory of her is practically seeing her heart breaking?"

Chaun silently nodded. "I had said it out of anger. It's a lesson I will carry until my dying day." Chaun looked down at the floor. "From now on, my words will be chosen carefully before I say them. I don't want to hurt anyone the way I hurt Kat that night. Like I told you, the guilt is overwhelming at times." He returned his gaze back to Jake. His eyes were stern and his face began to redden. Chaun's voice began to raise in decibel to match Jake's. "I loved her, even though I wasn't happy. I was so sick of her being so demanding of me all the time. She couldn't even ask me if she wanted something. You saw that before we left that night."

Jake's tone calmed. "What are you talking about?"

Chaun's tone didn't lower completely. "She told me to go get her coat and start the car. It wasn't, 'Chaun can you please get my coat for me and start the car?' No it was, 'Chaun, get my coat and go start the car.' I wasn't even able to finish my conversation. She rudely interrupted the conversation to demand what she wanted."

Jake nodded as he looked slightly to his left. "I remember hearing her say that."

"For the most part, our entire relationship was like that. She would demand and I would do it. I hardly stuck up for myself." He looked down at the cast on his foot, "Leave it to me to stick up for myself at the worst possible time."

Jake shook his head. "Chaun, there was no way for you to know what the outcome of that drive was going to be. That's why they call it an accident. You think everyday people go out knowing if they're going to wreck? The only exceptions are daredevils, stuntmen, and demolition derby contestants."

Chaun smirked, "Yeah, that's true. If I would have had any idea how events were to unfold, I would have at least sat in the car a couple more minutes before backing out of the driveway."

"I know you would have." Jake stood, reached out, and grabbed Chaun's shoulder. "I'm here for you if you need me. I might not be able to show up in person, but all you have to do is call."

Chaun nodded and his tone lowered. "Have you been by to see mom and dad yet?"

Jake shook his head. He grinned. "No, and if I know mom and dad, they will kick my ass if I don't. I'll, at least, give them a call on my way home. I'm going to head out for now. You get better bub, and I'll come by and see you after you get home."

Chaun nodded and smiled. "I will. Drive safe." Jake leaned over and hugged Chaun again.

"Will do" As Jake walked out of the room he said, "Take care."

#

Chaun sat in his hospital bed watching T.V. He had been surfing through the channels trying to find something interesting. After flipping twice through all the channels, he finally stopped on a show pertaining to medieval history. He looked at the clock on the wall. "One o'clock. Good, hopefully I've caught it at the beginning."

Even though the door was open, Chaun turned when a knock sounded throughout the room. Expecting to see family, friend, or nursing staff enter, he was shocked to see the Chaplain sheepishly poke his head around the corner. "Mr. Hutchins?"

Chaun gave a hesitant smile half expecting another outburst. "Chaplain Bishop?"

Charles stepped into the room and stood cowering. "I know I'm probably one of the last people that you want to see at the moment. Even though I had no control over what happened at our last meeting, I came by to apologize."

Chaun's eyebrow rose as with his intrigue. His hand motioned towards the chair next to his bed. Charles nodded and accepted Chaun's invitation.

Chaun looked into Charles' eyes, "What do you mean you had no control? Did you black out?"

"Kind of."

"How can there be an in between?"

Charles lowered his head gathering the words that would most accurately describe his experience. "Have you ever heard of a petit mal seizure?"

"No, I haven't. Are you saying your actions were due to a seizure?"

Charles shook his head. "No, but I believe it's the best way to explain what I experienced at our last meeting." Chaun nodded. "A petit mal is a seizure that causes its sufferer to stare absently for a given period of time. While seizing the person will sometimes be cognizant of what is going on around them while noticing they have no control of physical movements of their body. This is the best comparison to what I experienced during our last meeting. I was cognizant of what was happening, but was not able to control my movements or speech."

Chaun shook his head in disbelief. "Are you saying your body controlled itself?"

"No. I believe someone else was controlling my actions that day."

Chaun nodded. "Nice try Chaplain. I don't believe in ghosts or other dimensions." Chaun looked into Charles' eyes to find sternness.

"There is something else. I was shown a vision that day of the accident that put you here. The perspective was that of a passenger." Chaun's face went white as his mouth fell open. "Whether or not you believe in the paranormal Mr. Hutchins, it believes in you." Chaun nodded once again. "The real reason I came by, other than apologizing, was to see if I could give you any advice. I know you have got to be dealing with a lot after the shock you've had."

Chaun sat quiet for a moment looking into his lap. He nodded while raising his head to look at Charles once again. "Yes sir. I think in some ways the weight of the accident and loss has yet to fully sink in. I feel guilty about what was said. If your vision was accurate and your yelling made any sense, I'm pretty sure you know the gist of the conversation and words spoken just before the accident." Charles nodded. "How do I move on from that? It's not like I can snap my fingers and have all that regret gone. How can I make amends to someone that is gone?"

Charles shook his head. "I don't know. It sure won't be an easy road, but if you take it a day at a time and find the positives though out each day it may help with the slow process of healing. The staff told me your daughter survived the accident?" Chaun nodded as a tear rolled down his cheek. "Then allow her to be one of the positives from day to day. Her being alive is a miracle in itself. Healing after a loss and regret is a slow process and is never easy. Lean on those who love and cherish you, and they will make the road to healing less burdensome."

Chaun nodded again. "Thank you, sir. Your apology and advice is greatly accepted."

Charles smiled. "You're very welcome." He stood and shook Chaun's hand. "If you ever need to speak with me again just let the nursing staff know and I will be up at my earliest convenience.

"I will. Thanks again Charles."

#

The evening had been quiet. Dave had cooked dinner for Michelle and himself. They fed and spent time with Sam. Time had passed like it usually had since they brought Sam home. Their routine never changed much. As usual, they took Sam upstairs to lay her down for the night. Dave gently placed her in her crib and turned on the mobile above her crib. It played a lullaby as it quietly moved through its revolutions. Dave and Michelle never had a problem with Sam. On the rarity that she started fussing it was usually only for a few minutes. She slept through most of the night, only typically waking once or twice. Within a few minutes she was sleeping peacefully.

After Sam had gone to sleep, they went about their normal routine: changing into their sleepwear, brushing teeth, and taking meds. They both stayed up for a little while reading before going to sleep. About an hour and a half later, after both had just gone to sleep, a voice could be heard from the baby monitor. "Michelle, wake up. Michelle." The intensity of the voice rose. "Michelle. Michelle!"

Michelle raised her head from her pillow still half asleep, "What do you want?"

Dave mumbled, "I didn't say anything."

Michelle's head sank back into her pillow, "I must have been dreaming." The next second, at the sound of a door slamming in the house, both sat straight up in bed. "What was that?"

"I don't know. It almost sounded like a door slamming." Then the sound repeated. They looked at each other. "It sounded like it came from…" The panic of realization was immeasurable. Their faces were an agape, wide-eyed expression of mirrored terror. Both said at the same instant. "Sam's room." They scrambled out of bed and ran to the nursery. When they arrived, they realized that Sam was not breathing. Michelle ran to call 911. Dave began rescue breathing. He noticed the room had gotten very cold and the air thick and heavy.

Dave continued the rescue breathing until the paramedics arrived. They took Sam and Michelle in the ambulance. Dave followed in the Navigator. The paramedics got Sam breathing again before they arrived at the hospital.

The Dr. began running tests to see what had caused her to stop breathing. As the Dr. walked out of the room Dave stood and began to pace. His tone was a mixing pot of emotions. Some of which Michelle sensed, due to her feeling the same, were worry, terror, uncertainty, shock, and confusion. "That was really weird. Did you ask me what I wanted before the doors started slamming?"

"Yeah, I thought you had been calling my name."

"No, I was sound asleep until you rolled over and started asking me questions. He sat back down and looked at Michelle. His eyes were wide, mouth slightly agape. I think whoever was in the car with us on the way home from Ft. Wayne has become a guardian angel for Sam. I think that's who started slamming the door to her room."

Michelle's mouth dropped open and her face lengthened with revelation. "I think you're right. We would have never known until it was too late." She hugged Dave. Her hug was like a vice.

Dave wrapped his arms around her, looked down, and softened his voice. "No, we wouldn't have. Luckily someone is watching over Sam. I'm not sure if angel would be the right word, but it is definitely a guardian something. I don't think we should tell

Chaun about this just yet. At least not until he's home from the hospital. It would just cause him to worry and want to rush coming home."

Her grip finally easing, she released Dave, leaned back, and made eye contact. "I think you're right. He tends to worry a lot, especially when it involves family."

Dave nodded and placed his hand on hers. "Hopefully this is just a one-time incident."

A little while later the Dr. returned to the room. Dave and Michelle stood. Both wide eyed with hopeful curiosity. "Well it seems she is perfectly fine. I think, this may have just been a freak occurrence."

Dave's shoulders relaxed as he let out a deep sigh. "So, she's okay?"

The Dr. smiled, "I don't see anything wrong with the test results. She is healthy and all her numbers are fine."

Dave said, "Thank you, Dr."

"You're welcome. The nurse will be in shortly to have you sign the release paperwork." Dave nodded to let the Dr. know he understood.

Chapter 11

Chaun woke to the sound of footsteps entering his room. When he opened his eyes he saw Dr. Smith standing next to his bed. "Chaun?"

Chaun pushed himself up higher in the bed. "Morning Dr. Smith. What's up?"

"Not much, just came in to tell you the good news."

He sighed, expecting it would be more x rays, bloodwork, or therapy. "And what news might that be?"

He smiled, "Since you've done well over the last week with bearing weight on your leg, I've decided that you are ready to head home."

Chaun's face furrowed slightly. "You're not messing with me are you?"

Dr. Smith laughed. "Not this time. You should be able to leave as soon as you sign your paperwork and your parents come to pick you up."

Chaun's entire face lifted and lit up with excitement. "Thank you so much Dr. Smith. Are there any restrictions?"

The Doctor shook his head. "Not really. I've called and talked to your parents and they've bought a wheelchair for you to use for the next couple weeks. I want you to take it easy and don't overdo it." Chaun nodded to let the Dr. know he was listening. "Definitely work on building strength in that leg, but if it gets to the point it hurts more than stiffness or soreness stop."

Letting the Doctor's words sink in, Chaun nodded once more. "Gotcha, take it easy and don't overdo it. I won't have a problem with that. How soon before I get the other cast off?"

"It shouldn't be too much longer. We had to put a few pins in your bones due to where the breaks in your ankle were located. Your family Dr. can keep an eye on it. You should be able to remove it in a couple weeks or so. My guess would be at the outside two months as long as you take it easy and don't go trying to run any marathons or anything." He started laughing.

Chaun smirked. "Thanks Doc."

He smiled, "Not a problem. Any other questions?"

Chaun shook his head. "Nope, I'm good. Thanks again for everything."

"You're very welcome." Dr. Smith turned and left the room.

Denise entered the room a few minutes after the Dr. had finished speaking with Chaun. She was all smiles. She handed him a handful of papers. "Here are your release papers. All they need is your signature."

Chaun took the papers and pen. "Thank you."

Denise nodded, "You're welcome. I also called your parents to tell them the news. Your mom and Sam are on their way to pick you up."

He signed the papers and returned them to Denise. "Thanks again. I really can't wait to be home."

She gave the papers a quick look through to make sure everything was in order. She nodded, looked into Chaun's eyes, and smiled. "I'll bet. Most people take for granted being able to get up and move around, let alone go anywhere."

Chaun nodded then looked down. "That's true. I am going to miss having someone other than my parents to talk to." He returned his gaze to Denise. His face sad.

"You'll do fine. I'm sure you have people to call if you need to."

Chaun maintained eye contact while shaking his head. "Actually, I don't, most of the friends we hung out with were hers. My busy work schedule kept me from having too much of a personal life."

"Do you think your work schedule was the cause of how she treated you?"

"Treated me?" His brow subtly furrowed as he contemplated the answer. "No...added to the ill treatment, yes."

Denise looked down, "I didn't mean to offend you."

Chaun looked at her apologetically, "I wasn't offended. You just made me realize one of my shortcomings. All I can do is learn from it."

Her face lifted. She placed her hand on his shoulder. "Do you need any help packing up?"

"If you're not too busy. Granted, there isn't much to pack up." Chaun gave a slight laugh.

"That reminds me, your mom wanted me to let you know, she is bringing clothes for you to change into." Chaun started laughing at a chuckle and before too long was in stitches. "What's so funny?"

Chaun calmed himself just enough to speak audibly.

"So…am I to gather the staff prefers me not to leave in the nude?"

Denise started laughing, "That would be a sight. I can almost guarantee they won't prefer you leaving in the nude." Her laugh slowly subsided. "I'll help you get everything ready to go. I'm going to go and get this paperwork squared away and then I'll be right back.

#

An hour later Michelle walked into Chaun's hospital room pushing Sam in a stroller. "Is that a car seat that turns into a stroller?" Chaun's mouth hung open.

Michelle smiled and nodded, "Yeah, I really wish they would have had these when you were her age. It would have made our lives a lot easier. How are you feeling?" She walked over and gave him a hug.

"Really good. Do you have my clothes?"

She pulled a pair of jeans, socks, a black t-shirt, boxer briefs, and tennis shoes from a bag. "Here you go. That's what took me so long to get here. I had to stop by and pick these up for you."

"Thanks mom. Can you give me a few minutes while I change? I'll holler if I need anything." Michelle nodded her head and turned to leave the room. "Thanks mom." She closed the door behind her. Chaun found it surprisingly difficult to change. After putting the t-shirt on and the boxer briefs, he called his mom in to help him with the jeans.

After he was dressed, Denise brought in a wheelchair to escort him to the doors. His mom pushed the stroller alongside the wheelchair while they were on their way down to the first floor. Chaun held Sam's hand most of the way between his thumb and forefinger. As they got onto the elevator Denise asked Michelle, "How's Mr. Hutchins?"

She smiled and rolled her eyes jokingly. "He's good, been driving me nuts though the last few weeks."

Denise looked concerned, "Why's that?"

"He has been anxiously awaiting Chaun's release. They were always very close while Chaun was growing up. At times they were inseparable. Dave was one of Chaun's closest friends growing up. Most of that was due to moving around so much with Dave being in the Army."

Denise raised her head slightly. "I see. Does Chaun have anyone outside of the family to talk to if he gets bored?"

"He has a couple people, but most of his friends work during the week." Unbeknownst to Chaun Michelle handed Denise a piece of paper containing her phone number and e-mail address. The elevator toned and the metal door pulled back to reveal the floor they needed. They stepped off and walked towards the door. Michelle walked outside to pull the car up to the doors.

Denise said, "You know I tend to like a lot of my patients. No more than on a professional level of course. You I'm going to miss. I know some of the other girls are as well. Most of the people we deal with on a daily basis give us a little bit of hope. You on the other hand have impacted our lives. I hope you find peace, and know that you deserve it." She placed her hand on his shoulder.

He placed his hand on top of hers, "Thanks Denise."

Michelle pulled the car up in front of the doors. As she got out and started walking through the parting doors, Denise said to Chaun. "I guess this is good-bye."

"For now, at least. I'd say that good-byes aren't forever, but I know better. I hope we meet again someday. You helped me through a lot in the last few weeks. My day always seemed brighter on days you were working." His expression was somber with mental reflection. His voice soft.

Denise blushed slightly. Michelle came in and they pushed Sam and Chaun towards the doors to get them both in the car. As Michelle was getting Sam placed in the car, Denise was helping Chaun into the passenger seat. "Remember what the Dr. said, Take it easy and don't overdo it."

He smiled reflectively, "I will. You take care of yourself."

She nodded and then closed the door. Michelle waved to Denise as she started easing the car forward.

Chapter 12

It was not until they were South of Ft. Wayne that Michelle finally began speaking. Chaun spent most of that time staring off into space and enjoyed seeing anything other than hospital walls. "I have to admit, your father is excited to have you coming home."

With a light hearted tone he said, "Him? I've been going nuts staring at those hospital walls." Chaun looked at Michelle and grinned. He turned and looked out of his window again. He watched as they passed the barren branches of trees yet to spring forth new vegetation. He began to wish that he woke up a month later. Chaun longed for spring. He figured the chance to see new life would bury his guilt and the cold feelings of what happened the night of the accident. His mind drifted.

He sat in a coffee shop sipping his cup of coffee and studying for class. A woman at the table next to him kept looking his direction. Chaun looked up and smiled at the woman. She returned his smile. He looked back down and began to study again. The woman got up and walked over without his noticing. While he read he noticed the bottom hem of shorts and tan legs just beyond the table's edge. He raised his head to find that the young lady had walked over to his table. She was in her early twenties. "Is this seat taken?"

Chaun gestured to the open seat across from him, "Not at all."

She smiled and sat down. "I'm Katrina."

Chaun smiled and wondered if she was a hallucination. No one that beautiful had ever approached him. "Nice to meet you Katrina, I'm Chaun."

"I've always liked the name Chaun. S-E-A-N?" She looked down at his textbook. "What are you studying?"

"No. C-H-A-U-N. The Scottsboro trials that took place in the 1930's." Her face portrayed cluelessness. "It was a trial where nine African-American teenagers were wrongfully accused and tried for the rape of two white women."

She looked back up at him. Her face looked as if she was questioning his sanity. "Are you reading up on this for fun or for class?"

He smiled and was barely able to keep from laughing. He dog eared the page and closed the book. "Class, even though it is a pretty interesting subject. Not the rape part of it, but the process afterward and the story. I am a history major."

She nodded her head, "I see. How much longer do you have until you are finished?"

"About a year." He smiled and took a sip of his coffee. "I'm anxious to be done and working in the field."

"I'll bet." She leaned forward. "Chaun. Chaun. Chaun!" Kat's voice changed from hers to Michelle's. "Chaun!" He was back in the present, still looking out the window.

He sighed and blinked with the transition from memory to the present. "Yeah mom?"

"You okay? I started to get worried when you weren't responding to the conversation and weren't sleeping."

"I'm fine mom. I was just thinking of the day Kat and I met."

Michelle's voice and facial expression softened. "I'm sorry hon, how have you been doing with that issue lately?"

"Better than what I expected. It still hurts and I have my hard times, but I think it really hasn't sank in yet. I think once I get home and actually sit and have familiar surroundings it'll really hit." He looked down. Michelle glanced over and noticed he looked overwhelmed. His thoughts an unorganized mess. The only way to deal with them was as he came to them. "I've just had a lot going on the last few weeks. Between Drs. and nurses coming and going, you guys coming to visit before Sam left, and meeting Sam, I haven't had much time to focus on my feelings about that night."

Michelle reached over and placed her hand on Chaun's forearm. Her tone softened. "I understand, your father and I have a surprise for you."

Chaun looked up at Michelle. "What are you talking about?"

"Do you still like to read?"

Chaun began to laugh. He nodded, "Yeah mom, I still love to read." He thought that maybe they probably bought him a few books.

"We set up part of your room like a mini library. There's a chair and two full bookshelves lined with books."

Chaun's eyes widened. His voice excited. "You mean some of the three-foot bookshelves?"

Michelle shook her head and laughed. "No, the bookshelves are about six-foot-tall and three feet wide."

Chaun was stunned, "It would take me years to read that many books."

"We know, but we figured it would give you a variety to choose from. About a quarter of the books are children's literature. Your dad and I figured it'd be good quality time for you to read to Sam before bed every night."

Chaun's mouth closed. His eyes began to mist over. He looked back at Sam. With all the thoughts swimming through his head, none of them had been about him spending time with her. "Thank you. I will definitely choose a book off the shelf when I get home and set one aside to read to Sam tonight." He smiled at Michelle.

#

As they pulled in front of Dave and Michelle's home, Chaun was flooded with memories. There were so many times he hurt himself playing on the property. He remembered almost drowning in the pond towards the back of the property as well as sustaining that broken arm after falling out of the huge maple tree.

Dave stepped out onto the front porch as Michelle turned into the driveway. He was grinning from ear to ear as he walked closer to the car. Michelle shifted into park. Dave opened the hatch on the back of the Navigator and removed Chaun's wheelchair. Chaun noticed that they had installed a ramp leading to the front porch. After opening the wheelchair, Dave pushed it to the passenger door. He opened the door and helped Chaun out of the car. Chaun had never seen him this happy. Dave hugged Chaun with almost childlike enthusiasm. "How are you feeling son?"

"Good dad. I'm glad to be home." Chaun smelled a fragrance that was not normal for late winter. He looked around trying to pinpoint the location of the aroma. After he noticed it was coming from the direction of the house, he looked up at Dave, "Do I smell something grilling?"

Dave, still smiling, grabbed Chaun's shoulder. "Yep, I've prepared one of your favorite meals. I figured after eating hospital food for the last few weeks it would be a nice change. Not to mention it's been unseasonably warm this year." Chaun hadn't noticed until then but the temperature outside felt like it was middle to upper 60's. He nodded his head and looked around. For the most part, the grass was still brown. Here and there he could see a few hints of green blades trying to hide amid the dead brown. Dave pushed him up the ramp towards the front door.

"Did you put the ramp in?"

Dave laughed. "This time of year? Hell no. I hired someone to install it. I kept the receipt though to add to the cost of your care. Hell, even if the lawsuit fell through, I wouldn't have minded paying out of pocket for it." They entered the front door. Chaun was dumbfounded. They had installed a small elevator for him to get upstairs to his room. "We also had the elevator installed. I figured it would make it easier for you to get around, and we weren't sure how long you'd be in the chair."

Chaun's mouth fell open. "You didn't have to go to these extremes dad. One of the chair lifts on the stairs would have been sufficient enough. Thank you though, the gesture is much appreciated. Thank you also for letting me stay here until I recover."

Dave's voice softened. "You don't have to thank us Chaun. We did it because we love you and want your recovery to be as easy as possible." He pushed Chaun into the dining room and up to the table. "I'm going to leave you here for a few minutes. I have to go check on the food." He walked out of the sliding glass doors and up to the grill. Chaun could tell he was flipping something over. Dave walked back into the house.

Chaun never took his eyes off his dad. "Smells good, what are we having?"

Dave smiled. "Steak, I know it's always been one of your favorites."

Chaun grinned, "That it is. How've you been lately? I know we haven't had much chance to talk since you brought Sam home."

Dave sat down across from Chaun. He rested his hands on the table and interlaced his fingers. "I've been good. Staying busy getting things fixed up around here."

"That's good." Chaun looked out the window. The trees in the back yard were larger than they were when Katrina and he were dating. He thought back to when she loved to be among those trees. She had one in particular that she would sit under with a book and stay there most of the day. He remembered walking up numerous times as she sat reading in the shade. He remembered a few times watching her from inside the house. The trees around her changed from a vibrant green to brown and leafless. Dave was trying to get his attention. Katrina looked up and waved at him. Chaun blinked and she was gone.

Dave said, "You okay Chaun? You seemed like you were daydreaming or something."

Chaun blinked repeatedly to make sure the image was gone. "Something like that. I was just remembering when Kat used to sit under her favorite tree reading."

"Yeah, that was a more peaceful and happier time." Dave looked out at the trees then back at Chaun. He tapped the table between them to gain Chaun's attention. "How are you holding up with everything?"

Chaun looked at Dave and shrugged. "Good, I guess. That has been the second time today that I've remembered times with Kat in the past. Maybe it's my way of finally beginning to cope with her loss and moving past it. Maybe I'm trying to reflect on the happier times to experience stronger feelings regarding her death. I have unspeakable guilt about what was said. Her heartbroken face haunts me. I see it often. Maybe the news hasn't sank in due to all the pain she put me through while we were together." He looked down at the table and shook his head. "There has just been so much to take in after waking from the coma: The accident, losing Kat, Sam, my injuries, rehab, and the lawsuit. It's just so much to sort through."

Dave's voice was soft. "Chaun, look at me." Chaun made eye contact. "I know it seems overwhelming. We're here to help anyway we can." Chaun nodded. "I know you feel guilty about that night. You're not heartless. A heartless person would have no remorse." He looked down at his hands. His tone was serious. "I think you're right though, the happier times are the ones you will miss. Even though you feel guilt over what you said and the expression on her face, you have got to move on." Chaun lowered his gaze to the table as Dave got up to check on the steaks again.

Chapter 13

Dave walked down the stairs. It was morning. Michelle was up and Dave's nose told him that she had made coffee. He walked into the kitchen to find that she was sitting at the island reading a book. She looked up at him and smiled. "Morning sweetie…coffee's fresh if you want any."

"Morning hon." He walked over and kissed her on the cheek.

She smiled and whispered, "We are having company later today."

Dave looked at her and smirked. "Oh really? And whom are we expecting?" He opened the cupboard to get his favorite coffee cup. It was camouflage with the Army Master Sergeant chevron on the side of the cup.

"A certain nurse from the hospital. It's a surprise, so Chaun isn't to know."

Dave's smirk changed to a smile. "Would that by chance be Ms. Parker?" Michelle nodded her head in response. "That's great. How has she been?"

"Good. She's anxious about coming by today." She looked at Dave and smiled.

"That's good to hear. What time are we to expect her?"

Michelle looked at the clock on the stove. "I told her noon would be fine."

Dave poured his coffee. "Sounds good. I can cook up some grilled chicken or ribs for dinner. I'll have to see what she prefers."

Michelle took a sip of her coffee. "Sounds like a plan. I'm wondering how excited Chaun's going to be when she shows up."

Dave shrugged his shoulders. "Time will tell."

As agreed, Denise showed up a few minutes before noon. Michelle went out to greet her. Due to the warmer than usual weather for being the beginning of April, Dave sat out on the patio with Chaun. Chaun had his back to the sliding glass door. The sliding glass door opened and Denise stepped through it. Thinking it was Michelle, Chaun didn't bother turning. She walked up behind Chaun, put her head next to Chaun's to where her mouth was right by his ear, and whispered, "Boo." Chaun was so startled that he almost toppled the wheelchair.

Denise could tell when he turned around that he was almost as surprised to see her. He was all smiles. "What are you doing here?"

She hugged him and smiled in return. "Your mom thought it would be a nice surprise if I came down to visit for a while. She figured it would give you someone besides them to visit with."

Chaun looked at Michelle. "Thanks mom. You didn't have to set this up, but thank you."

Denise's brow furrowed and her eyes told Chaun she seemed slightly offended. "What do you mean?"

"I mean I don't mind spending time with you. It's been nice without Katrina here dominating the conversation." He looked at Denise. "Don't take it like I don't want you here. I do. I'm overjoyed you wanted to come and see me. It means a lot to me."

Denise blushed, "Thanks Chaun. I wanted to visit sooner, but I have been busy at work lately. I do have the next few days off though."

Chaun smiled, "That's good to hear."

"Maybe you can crash here tonight since you don't have to work in the morning." Chaun and Denise looked up at Michelle in shock, then back at each other.

She gently bit her bottom lip while looking at Chaun questioningly. She released her lip from its ivory clamp. "If Chaun's okay with it, I can."

Chaun shook his head and smiled. "I don't mind at all. Then you wouldn't have to try and drive back to Ft. Wayne tired as hell."

"Well we will go in the house and let you two talk for a while." Dave said as he stood up to walk into the house.

"Thanks dad." Chaun watched as they walked into the house. Once the door was closed, he looked at Denise. "How have you been?"

"Good." She placed her hand on top of his then removed it. "How are you holding up? Has everything fully hit you yet?"

He tilted his head a little to the right. "Yes and no. It's still hit and miss. I have good days and bad days."

"That's weird, it should have sank in by now." Her look curious as if she was trying to mentally run through reasons why

Chaun had not responded to his past. "Do you have any idea why it hasn't?"

Chaun shook his head and shrugged his shoulders. "Not a clue. I've been thinking about it for the last month. I'm wondering if part of it was my being miserable most of the time while in the relationship. I didn't want to break her heart, but I wasn't happy." His expression grew distant. "What I said to her that night can't be taken back and the last look I remember on her face can't be erased from memory. Granted what I said was mostly out of frustration, but still I did mean part of it." He looked towards the trees as his voice quieted. "I realize that now."

"Yeah." Denise's voice was soft and understanding. "If you need anything when it fully hits, I'm only a phone call away. Even if it's in the middle of the night, I'll be free to talk." She patted his forearm. "Hell, if you need me to, I'll drive down from Ft. Wayne just so you can have a shoulder to cry on."

"Thanks Denise." He grinned. "Do you do this for all your patients?"

She smiled. "No, I would never do this for a patient."

He gave a questioning look. "Then why the special attention for me?"

"When you awoke in your room that day, I saw something in your eyes. There was genuine character that I wanted to understand deeper. More on a friendship level than anything more." He looked into her eyes. Her voice completely serious and reassuring. "I wouldn't try to pursue you for more than that, unless later on down the road it happens that way. Your eyes just told a story of depth that I thought would be interesting to know."

Chaun shook his head. In that moment his respect for Denise was exponential. "Thanks for that. I haven't received a compliment that nice in years. What would you like to know?"

She shook her head. "What do you mean?"

"You said you would like to get to know me more, which I took as pick my brain to see what I knew." He smiled. He tapped his fingertips on the table. "As far as the genuine character, that will have to be shown through interaction over time."

"I also could tell by looking at you that you were more intelligent than you let on." She made eye contact and noticed Chaun's coy grin. "How smart are you?"

"My I.Q. was 131 fresh out of high school. What it is now after college and years more of learning, I couldn't tell you."

She sat mouth agape and wide eyed. "Wow, that's almost genius level."

Chaun grinned, "Yeah, but don't tell anyone. I like to keep that under wraps. The reaction when someone finds out is priceless."

Denise started laughing. "I can see why. Is there any particular subject you are more knowledgeable in than others?"

Chaun tilted his head left and then brought it back to center. "Other than history, it's pretty much even. For the most part I don't know a lot about a little, but a little about a lot."

"You know that could be dangerous on certain levels."

He laughed. "Yeah that's true, but on the bright side it does make it helpful at times. I've been told I'm a plethora of useless information." Chaun laughed slightly. "One of the things I love most is knowing trivia or random facts."

"I can see where that would be helpful." Her brow lowered. "Remind me never to play against you in a game of trivia."

Dave opened the door. Denise and Chaun turned their heads to look at him. "Dinner is almost ready. I already have the table set up."

"Thanks dad." Denise pushed Chaun into the house and up to the dining room table.

Chapter 14

Throughout the next month, Denise would visit regularly. The more she visited the more the family started noticing more activity from the entity. Items around the house would seem to get misplaced. They would turn up someplace totally out of the ordinary, only to be found a few days to a week later.

At first, it led to a few arguments between Chaun, Dave, and Michelle. On certain occasions one would accuse another of moving or misplacing items. Due to not knowing about Sam's trip home from the hospital and the incident when she stopped breathing, Chaun believed it was Dave and Michelle moving items. Dave and Michelle slightly suspected that it was the entity moving items around to cause chaos among the household. Dave set up a video camera in the living room to see if he could by chance, catch the culprit in the act. He did not tell Michelle, Chaun, or Denise. Dave placed the camera on top of the dining room table facing into the living room. The only entrance into the area that was not visible was the kitchen. He made sure the night mode was set and went to bed.

Dave woke and walked downstairs to the kitchen. He got his cup and poured his coffee. Michelle said, "Why was the camcorder on the entertainment center and left on?"

"I left it out to see if I could catch whoever was moving things around the house." He paused for a second. Dave looked down at his coffee cup then back up at Michelle in disbelief. "Where did you say you found it?"

"The entertainment center in the living room."

Dave's jaw dropped as he walked to the hallway. He looked down the hallway at the entertainment center in the living room. No camera. "Where is it?" Dave had an urgency in his voice.

"It's back in the closet and the battery is on the charger." Dave ran to the closet and yanked the camera off the shelf. He ran back into the kitchen and grabbed the battery off the charger. He quickly inserted the battery into the camcorder and turned it on anxious to view the footage. Michelle watched him the entire time. His actions began to worry her. "Why are you so fidgety?"

He stared at the camera display with complete concentration. "I didn't place the camera on the entertainment center." He quickly scanned through the footage to see when the camera started moving.

Michelle's brow furrowed. She shook her head not believing what she had heard. "Where did you leave it then?"

He turned the viewing screen towards Michelle. "On the dining room table." Michelle's mouth dropped open as she watched footage of the camera moving from the dining room table. It rotated as it was transferred from its spot of origin to its place of rest. As the camera was set down, it showed Denise still sound asleep on the couch. As Dave looked over the footage, he believed it was not someone human moving the camera. Yet, the kitchen was not visible from where he had initially set up the camera. He decided he would try it again that night, and he would strap the camera down to where someone would have to undo the straps in order to move it.

That night he set up the camera to where all entrances into the room were visible. Dave placed a strap down over the camera holding it in place. He went to bed. He awoke the next morning to find the camera still in place. He unstrapped the camera and took it into the kitchen. He took out the battery and placed it on the charger. He made a pot of coffee and fixed a cup when it was finished brewing. Dave took the battery out of the charger and placed it in the camera. He sat down at the island and turned on the camera to view the footage.

Dave watched in awe as not one item over the course of the video was moved around the living room, but three. No one entered or exited the living room. The items seemed to hover in midair from one location to another. Strangely enough, all three items were stacked on top of one another on the entertainment center. Dave rushed into the living room and retrieved the items. The three items were: a DVD of Payback, a picture of a heart with the frame shattered, and a clock that had been hanging on the wall. He pondered as to why those three items were chosen to be moved. He set them down on the island, sat down, and drank his coffee while pondering the meaning of the message. The heart was easy, but why the other two? He couldn't wrap his mind around it.

Michelle walked down the stairs in her bathrobe shortly after he sat down. She walked over and kissed him on the cheek. "Why do you have the stuff set out?"

Dave picked up the camera and showed her the footage. "These were the items that were moved?" Dave kept looking at the items trying to solve the puzzle.

She looked at the objects and then back at Dave. "What do they mean?"

"That's what I can't figure out. The heart of course means a broken heart, but the others…their meaning eludes me."

She patted his shoulder. "You'll figure it out." She kissed his forehead. "You're one of the smartest people I know." She walked over and fixed her cup of coffee.

Chapter 15

Dave, Michelle, Chaun, and Sam arrived at the courthouse 15 minutes early. Their hearing was at two o'clock in the afternoon. On the phone, Chris sounded hopeful that things would work out. He had said they had some things to discuss before the hearing. If they arrived five to ten minutes early it should be enough time to talk things over. As they got onto the elevator Dave said to Chaun, "You okay with all this?"

Chaun's face looked exhausted and worn. He nodded. His voice sounded tired and worried. "Yeah, just hoping they don't run us through a lengthy court process. It is bad enough I have to remember that night over and over again. I don't much like the idea of having to sit and talk about it in front of total strangers."

Dave looked down towards the floor for a second, then back up at Chaun. He reached out and laid his hand on Chaun's shoulder. "I understand son. It will all be over soon enough."

When the doors opened, they saw Chris waiting outside the courtroom. His face brightened when he saw them. As he approached, he said, "You're early."

"I prefer to typically be punctual by at least a few minutes."
Dave said.

Chris quickly pursed his lips, shrugged his shoulders, and
tilted his head. "That's never a bad thing. If you will follow me we
can talk things over in private." Chris led the family down the
hallway to an office that was just a small room of probably twelve
foot by twelve foot in dimension. Chaun noticed Chris' height for
the first time. When Chris arrived when Chaun was in the hospital,
Chaun could tell he was short, but now standing next to him he
realized he had to be five foot tall at the most. Chris led the family
into the room and motioned for all of them to have a seat. As they sat
down Chris looked concerned when he began to talk, "I've got good
news and possibly bad news." Chaun's brow furrowed and his tone
grew more worried, yet slightly angered. "The good news is that the
company has decided to settle. The bad news is that the amount is
not what I was hoping for."

Chaun's brow raised closer to normal once Chris told them
the news. "The amount doesn't matter. No amount will bring her
back. At minimum as long as they settle for enough to pay off the

hospital bills and some of Sam's care, that's really all I care about. You were asking for what, five?"

Chris nodded. "That's correct. Granted it's more than what you really need but I was thinking of Sam's college and cost of living for the rest of her life…and yours." Chris looked down at his papers then back up at Chaun. "They've agreed to three million."

Chaun's eyes widened and his mouth hung open. He thought, when Chris negotiated with the company that the total would get hacked down to well below five million dollars. "Three million!?"

Chris smiled and nodded. "Yeah."

Chaun shook his head. "That's more than what we need, but like you said if it pays for Sam to go to a decent college and be taken care of the rest of her life then it should be sufficient. The Doctor bills are, at least, a couple hundred thousand. It's not cheap being stuck in a hospital bed for two months."

Chris' brow furrowed. "I'm sure it isn't. With what they've agreed to, you will have the choice of not going back to work and spending more time with Sam."

Chaun nodded, "That is true. If you're asking if I agree to the amount, I don't. But, if it's what they are offering, I'll accept it."

Chris smacked the table. "Good. If everyone will follow me we can head down to the meeting room. Since the company has agreed to settle, we will not be meeting in the court room." Chris rose, along with the family, and led them to a much larger room with a long conference table. The walls were lined with bookshelves packed with reference books and ledgers. At the head of the table sat a man with blonde hair who looked to be about 50. To his right sat a man who looked 45. He had black hair and he was constantly looking down at the table. To his right sat a woman who appeared to be in her mid-thirties with blonde hair and blue eyes.

The man at the head of the table spoke with a deep voice that almost startled Chaun. "If everyone would please take a seat, so we can get started." His voice seemed distant, like he had a long day and was just going through the motions until he was able to go home. The family and Chris took their seats. As soon as everyone was seated the judge spoke again, "Well if we're ready to begin. Ms. Springer, I believe your client has offered a settlement?"

The woman nodded and said flatly, "That's correct your Honor."

The Judge looked at Chris, "Mr. Hastings, have you spoken to your client about the offered settlement?"

Chris answered, "Yes I have your Honor. He agrees to the offered settlement. Here is the paperwork. A copy was sent to Ms. Springer's office." Chris handed the paperwork to the Judge, who looked it over and then passed it on to the Defense Attorney.

The entire time, his shoulders remained hunched over the table. His voice stayed almost monotone. "Ms. Springer, did you receive and read over the paperwork?"

Her tone still mimicked the Judge's, as if both were just going through the usual formalities. "Yes, your honor."

As he slid the paperwork across the table he said, "Are these the documents you received?"

Her expression remained bland as she reviewed the paperwork and nodded her approval. "Yes, your honor."

The Judge gave a single nod then looked around the table as he said, "Good, if we can get all parties to sign the document then we can get it notarized and be done." Everyone then signed the document one by one. The judge then handed it to the notary who then walked out for a few minutes, notarized the document, and returned. "Well that is that. Now if everyone will excuse me, I have another case to preside over in about ten minutes."

As they were leaving the company owner approached Chaun. "Mr. Hutchins." Chaun turned and looked at the man as he approached. He was around 5' 8" tall. "I just wanted to tell you, that I know no amount of money will bring back your wife. I can only give you my heartfelt apology and condolences. I can also tell you that the man driving that truck that night was fired for his carelessness."

The man was surprised to see Chaun's face portray understanding. Chaun's tone was soft and contained, not malice but gratitude. "Thank you for your condolences. You are right. No amount of money will bring Katrina back, but it will be helpful in paying off the doctor bills from the accident as well as give Sam a good education and future." The two shook hands and went their separate ways.

Chris approached Chaun and the family. "Now all you have to do is wait. My office will handle all the details. If you don't have an investment account, we can give you places that will accept monetary amounts as large as what you'll be receiving. If you open an account with an investment company just call or come by the office with the details of the account."

Chaun said to Chris as he shook his hand, "Thank you. I actually am getting ready to go across the street to the investment company there and open an account."

"You're welcome. Just call or come by the office and give us the account information so we know where to send the settlement."

"I'll do that, thanks again." Chris nodded his head as he walked away.

Chapter 16

Denise and Chaun sat on the outside patio with Dave and Michelle. The sun had nearly set and the four sat at the table with a few candles and the dining room lights for illumination. Dave and Michelle stood up. "Well, I think we're going to turn in for the night. It's been a long day." Dave said.

"Night mom and dad. Love you guys."

"Goodnight Chaun, love you to." They both said in unison.

Denise smiled at Dave and Michelle. "Goodnight guys." Denise said.

"Goodnight sweetie." Michelle said. She gave a slight grin. "Don't keep him up too late."

"I'll try not to." Denise smiled. After Dave and Michelle had gone into the house, she looked at Chaun. Her smile softened as she placed her hand on Chaun's. "Haven't had much time to talk with you one on one like this for a while. How are you doing?"

Chaun looked at her hand covering his. His brow raised. Chaun thought for a second and realized she was right. "Man, it has been a while. I'm doing okay. I still can't believe it's the middle of

June already. One problem I've been having since the accident is trouble sleeping at night. I don't know why, but I don't sleep as well as I did before the accident."

She rested her elbow on her knee. Her head she rested on her hand. "Is it due to your feelings about that night?"

Chaun shook his head. "No, actually it's not. That's what has been bugging me about it. I don't think it's due to the guilt."

She squinted, looked down to her left, and then back at Chaun. "It might be the lack of having someone in the bed next to you. I've heard that people, after sleeping with someone else in the bed for so long, sometimes have problems sleeping without someone next to them."

Chaun looked at Denise slack jawed. Chaun's eyes widened with the realization. "I'll be damned. That's exactly it. I have felt like something has been off, since the accident, which has been causing my poor sleep. It didn't even dawn on me that it was not having someone next to me." Chaun quieted. He looked at Denise with a hopeful look in his eyes. "Would you be willing to sleep with me tonight and see if it helps? I promise I won't try anything more than just sleeping."

Denise sat back, smiled, and chuckled. She nodded. "Sure, I'd love to crash in your room tonight. That couch is getting more uncomfortable with each passing night. I also want you to know that I won't make any kind of moves on you as well. I want you to take things at your own pace."

Chaun smiled reflectively, "Thank you for that." He looked up at the stars. "They're gorgeous. Don't you think?"

Denise looked up. "That they are. I always love looking at them when I have time. Oh look, a shooting star. It's strange, I've always wondered…how can a star fall?"

Chaun chuckled, "They don't. Actually, what people call shooting stars are just meteors entering Earth's atmosphere."

She looked at his surprised face. "Really? I never knew that. Interesting. Are you finally glad to be out of the wheelchair?"

Chaun smiled and looked down to reassure himself that he was finally out of the chair. "Very. I was getting sick of having to have someone push me around or wheel myself around." Chaun inspected his chest and arms. "On the other hand, it did help me get a little more tone on my upper body." He started laughing. "Maybe I should keep it and use it for regular workouts."

Denise laughed. "That or you could always just start lifting and working out." Denise smiled. "How are you adjusting to not having to work ever again?"

"Decently, I guess. I don't have to worry about punching a clock and I get to spend all the time I want with Sam, my family, and the few friends I do have." His expression and tone softened. "I have to thank you."

Her eyes narrowed. "Thank me? For what?"

"For being such a good friend and always going out of your way to help me and make sure I'm doing all right."

Denise smiled, "You don't have to thank me for anything. I do what I do because I care." She placed her hand on his arm. "Like I told you before there was something special about you that I wanted to know on a personal level. A level I wouldn't have gotten to know just in the short time you were at the hospital." Chaun's eyes started growing heavy. Denise could tell he was fighting sleep. "You wanting to head up to bed?"

Chaun nodded his head. His eyes widened as he inhaled deeply. "Yeah that would be good. I'm not too bashful so just sleep however you're comfortable."

Denise grinned. "I'm not fully comfortable around you yet to sleep how I normally sleep. I also don't think your parents would appreciate it if I slept how I normally do."

Chaun smiled. "And how's that?"

She blushed and looked at the ground. "In the nude."

Chaun's eyes widened, he blushed, and laughed. "I can see where that would be a problem. I also know if you slept like that I may try and rush things. It has been a while."

Denise blushed and smiled. "And that's why I'm going to sleep in a t-shirt and my underwear." The two got up, walked inside, and climbed the stairs to bed.

Chapter 17

The next morning, as usual, Dave and Michelle were in the kitchen drinking coffee. Dave sat at the island and Michelle stood by the counter. "Did Denise go home last night?" Michelle asked then sipped her coffee.

Michelle saw one side of his mouth raise to form a proud half smile. "No, she slept in Chaun's room last night."

Michelle smiled, "That's good. I have to admit I really do like her." Her mouth leveled as she quickly thought of the adequate words to describe her perception of Denise. "She seems so caring and genuine."

"I couldn't agree more." Dave smiled. He looked at Michelle over the rim of his coffee cup. "I really hope it's the start of something between them." He set his cup down on the island. Dave stared at it for a moment. When he looked back at Michelle his face portrayed sincerity. "I loved Katrina, but Chaun seems more like himself around Denise. He always seemed different around Kat."

Michelle had noticed Chaun's adjusted behavior years before while he was with Katrina. She looked down at the coffee in her cup.

Her expression told Dave she was reliving the painful reality of Chaun choosing to be someone else to please Kat. She had internally struggled with this issue for years. "It was like he had to be someone else around her to keep her happy. I think Denise is a good match for him…and they would make a cute couple." They both turned to look towards the staircase as footsteps rang out in the foyer. Dave gave Michelle a questioning look when they realized that the walking noise sounded slow, as if the person was walking with a limp. Denise came into view. As she walked down the stairs, they noticed she was favoring her left leg. Michelle walked to the foot of the staircase. She looked up at Denise through furrowed brow and squinted eye. "You okay sweetie?"

"Yeah. My leg got scratched somehow." Denise finally made it to the foot of the stairs and Michelle walked with her into the kitchen and had her sit down next to Dave. "It may have been Chaun scratching me with his foot." She lifted her left leg back for Michelle to inspect it. She winced. Her mouth fell open at the sight of four scratch marks, side by side, that were at least six inches long.

Michelle looked at her calf. "Chaun couldn't have, he is meticulous about his nails. He always keeps them clipped and filed. It doesn't look like the skin is broken. I'll get some ice for it."

Denise looked up just as Michelle began walking towards the refrigerator. "Thanks Michelle."

"You're welcome." Michelle went to the freezer and retrieved an ice pack. She then pulled a dishtowel from a drawer next to the sink, and handed the icepack to Denise. "How'd you sleep last night?" Her face was set with a slight grin.

Denise gave a short uncomfortable laugh. "It's not how it appeared. Chaun said he hasn't been sleeping well since the accident and asked if I'd stay in his room to see if it would help him sleep." Denise shifted her gaze between Michelle and Dave. She held up her hands, the icepack still clutched in her left. "Nothing happened other than sleeping. I told him last night that I would take things at his pace. I wouldn't make any advances if he wasn't ready."

Michelle and Dave both looked at each other and smiled. Dave then looked at Denise. "That's very admirable. I like that you are willing not to take things too fast."

Michelle looked at Denise. She stepped toward Denise and placed her hand on Denise's shoulder. "I am glad you decided to keep contact after he was released from the hospital. Dave and I were just talking about the situation."

Denise's brow furrowed inquisitively. "The situation?"

Michelle removed her hand from Denise's shoulder, walked to the other side of the island, and took a sip of her coffee. She looked up and smiled at Denise. "Yeah. Since you have been coming by, we've noticed Chaun is more open and himself around you." Her smile sank to a frown. "When Kat was around, he acted like someone else. It was like he had to be someone else around her to make her happy. We loved Kat, but we could tell it was hard for Chaun to be with her. He didn't seem truly happy when he was with her."

Denise's brow remained furrowed, but her eyes transitioned from questioning to sadness. "I hate that he had to experience that. No one should have to change to make another person happy. Especially when that person is their spouse."

Dave turned the page on his paper. "I couldn't agree more."

They all heard footsteps coming down the stairs. All three turned their heads to see Chaun walk down the stairs and enter the kitchen.

"Morning everyone." He saw Denise holding the cold compress on her leg. He rushed over to Denise. His brow rose and his eyes widened when she removed the cold compress to reveal the scratches. "What happened?"

She looked at him still in total confusion as to how the scratches were left on her leg. "I don't know. I somehow got scratched during the night."

"Have you still been clipping and filing your nails?" Michelle asked. Her tone, calm.

Chaun looked up at her and nodded. "Religiously. You know I've always been compulsive about my nails. I can't stand having jagged edges on them." Chaun looked at the scratch marks on Denise's leg again. "I don't think toenails did this. The spacing is too far apart."

Dave looked down at Denise's calf. His brow rose and his lips pursed. "He's right. Those scratch marks aren't close enough together to have been made by toes. Did you scratch or claw at something on your leg last night?" Dave looked up and made eye contact with Denise.

She shook her head. "No, I slept sound through the night. Speaking of which...," she looked at Chaun, "How did you sleep last night?"

Chaun looked up at her. He tilted his head and nodded. "Better than I have in a long time. I haven't told anyone else before, but I've been waking up since the accident with horrible nightmares." He looked at Denise. "I didn't lie to you last night though, I do think that not having someone there was making the sleepless nights worse. Not having someone there was adding to the stress from the nightmares." He patted her hand. "Having you next to me was comforting. Thank you."

She placed her hand on the side of his face. A soft frown caressed hers. "You're welcome. Why didn't you tell anyone about the nightmares?"

Chaun looked at everyone in the room. "I knew everyone was stressed and worried enough. I didn't want to make it worse."

Dave gently grabbed Chaun's shoulder. "Son, that's why we are here. If you're having problems let us know about them so we can help you. We want you to be as stress free as possible. You don't have to live in fear or worry around us." Dave said.

"Thanks dad." He looked back at Denise apologetically. "I should have said something earlier."

She leaned in closer to him while nodding her head. "Yes you should have, that's why I've been asking you how you've been doing. I've been around for you to confide in if it was needed. That includes nightmares or anything that may seem minor. I want you to feel free to tell me anything."

Chaun stood up and hugged Denise. "Thank you, and I'll do my best to be more open…" He released Denise and looked at his parents. He looked at Dave and Michelle. "with everyone."

Sam began to cry. "I'll go get her." Michelle said. As she walked upstairs the three left the kitchen and sat down in the living room.

Chapter 18

Michelle walked into the living room carrying Sam. She laid out a baby blanket on the floor and placed Samantha on it. She sat down in her usual chair and looked at Chaun and Denise. "Are you guys dating or getting serious? You guys would make a really cute couple."

Denise blushed a bit. She looked at Chaun. They both shook their heads. "No. Last night was just to see if having someone with him would help him sleep."

"I agree with your mom. You two would make a wonderful couple. Honestly Chaun, you've needed someone like Denise all along," Dave held his hands up to show he meant no offense. "but that's just my opinion."

Chaun smiled. "I have to agree dad. I have needed someone like Denise for a long time. She has told me though that she will take things in my time. She won't make a move unless I do first."

Michelle smiled, "That's good and very respectable."

Denise gave a sheepish smile. "Thank you, Michelle. I know if I take things on my time and rush Chaun, it may cause problems later on."

"That's true. It is always good to take your time at these things anyways." Michelle crossed her arms as she started shivering. "Did someone turn the temperature down on the thermostat?" She looked as everyone one of the others shook their heads. In her peripheral vision she caught sight of something unnatural. Michelle turned her head to see Sam sitting in the middle of the living room floor unassisted. Those dark irises stared back at her once again. Her breath misted the atmosphere in front of her face. "Denise, please refresh my memory. It isn't normal for a six-month-old baby to sit on their own is it?"

All four stared at Sam. Their faces portrayed absolute shock. Though only seen through everyone's peripheral vision, she shook her head. No one could take their eyes off of Sam. The eyes that looked back at everyone bore black orbs on white almond shaped canvass. The skin tone around Sam's eyes and on her cheeks were dark grey. "No. She shouldn't be sitting unassisted for at least another month or two."

Michelle's mouth, like everyone else's, hung open. "That's what I thought. Dave, the eyes are exactly like they were before."

"I see that Michelle." Dave pushed the feeling of shock to the back of his mind. He leaned forward attempting to take control of the situation. He hoped the others would follow his example and find strength to take charge in the situation. "Who are you and what do you want?"

The voice that emanated from Sam made Chaun and Denise gasp. It was the same stammering, high pitched voice that Dave and Michelle heard in the car the day they brought Sam home from the hospital. "Who I am... is not important. You... will know that... when I decide it's time. I... am here... for retribution." Sam's head turned towards Chaun. Whoever was in Sam appeared to be staring into the depths of Chaun's soul. Chaun was paralyzed. No matter how hard he tried, he could neither move nor look away. Only the feeling of immense fear held him in place.

Dave spoke again, "Was it you that moved the items onto the entertainment center?"

The head turned and the eyes bore into Dave's. "Yes."

Dave nodded while mentally running through the right questions to ask. "What was the significance?"

"That… you will know… when I reveal my identity." She turned back to Chaun. "Moving objects… are only the beginning. I will make you suffer… far more… than just discomfort."

Denise spoke up. "Was it you that scratched me?"

Sam snapped her gaze to Denise, her mouth open. The sound she released was half snarl half hiss. The lights dimmed and frost began to form on the glass objects throughout the room. "Shut up! You… are nothing more… than a slut. Don't speak to me. You're only after Chaun… for his money… nothing more."

"That's not true." Denise was beginning to cry and cower at the rage of the entity. Denise crossed her arms, hugging her stomach.

Sam growled, "Silence! This is everyone's warning…I will not ease up. I will make your lives… a living hell… until I see fit that vengeance has been redeemed."

Michelle said, her voice trembling, "Why have you chosen to possess the baby?"

Sam looked at Michelle. Her face relaxed and a softer, much calmer tone. "She… is the easiest way… to speak with everyone at once. You can rest assured Michelle… the baby will be unharmed. As much as I want my vengeance… I will bring no harm… to this child." The entity laid down on the floor, the room warmed to the normal temperature that Dave and Michelle usually kept it, and Sam was moving sporadically like a normal baby of six months. Dave stood up and walked over to Samantha. He looked down to find her normal blue eyes looking up at him.

Chapter 19

The Entity made good on its promise. Over the following weeks, items, instead of just being relocated, were thrown and broken. The scratching increased. Dave and Michelle had a party for the fourth of July. It was just the family. Denise was technically the only other person outside of family present. Denise arrived about five in the evening. Michelle met her at the door and helped her carry the food items she was carrying in from her car.

She smiled at her as she grabbed one of the bags. "You didn't have to bring anything."

Denise closed the front door with her elbow. "I wanted to."

"It looks delicious. What is the dessert?" Michelle said as she set the container on the island.

"It has whipped cream, angel food cake, French vanilla pudding, and crushed peanut butter candy bars." She grinned.

Michelle stared at the dessert drooling. "That sounds divine. How are things going? I know we don't get to talk a lot woman to woman." Michelle leaned against the counter and Denise against the island. "Coffee? Dave drinks it at any time of day."

Denise glanced at the coffee pot then back at Michelle. "Yes, please. I'm doing well. I've been thinking of looking for a job closer to here, but it seems like no one in this area is hiring."

Michelle poured the coffee and handed Denise the cup. "Yeah, jobs aren't the greatest in this area. That's why Chaun had to go all the way to Indianapolis when he was working. Most of the museums around here are volunteer. She sighed and smiled sarcastically. The joys of small-town life. How are you and Chaun doing? He really doesn't talk much about it."

Denise seemed to light up. She nodded, smiled, and stood up straighter. "We're doing good, still taking it slow. Other than cuddling in bed, the most he does is hold my hand while we're out."

"Well that's good," Denise frowned. Michelle placed her hand on Denise's arm. "just give him time sweetie. He'll come around sooner or later."

Denise nodded and leaned back against the island. "I know he will. We really haven't talked about the issue."

Michelle grinned, "Like I said hon, just give it time. I know Dave's been hinting at him. Dave thinks that Chaun may be hesitant to move on so soon after Kat's death. He thinks that it may add to Chaun's guilt and make it look like he really didn't love her."

Denise looked down at the floor and nodded her head sullenly. "That would make sense. I've kind of got that impression of him over the last few months. I can tell he's wanting to, but he's holding back." She looked up at Michelle. She gave Michelle a forced smile as a tear rolled down her cheek. "I will continue to give him time." She wiped the tear from her cheek. "He'll take the next step when he's ready. He's worth the wait."

Michelle stepped over to Denise and hugged her. After a moment she stepped back. "Well that's all you can do. Let's go see what the boys are up to. They are out on the patio." Michelle walked out of the kitchen as Denise followed. As they stepped out onto the patio Michelle looked at Dave. "Do you need anything from inside?"

"No, I'm good." Dave looked up and smiled when he saw Denise. "Hey, Denise. How are you?"

She forced a smile. "I'm good. How are you?"

"Couldn't be better." Dave winked at her.

Denise walked up and hugged Chaun from behind while he was still in the chair. "Hey you."

He reached up and touched Denise's arm. "Hey. Have a good drive here?" Chaun asked.

"Yep, I sure did."

"That's good. You ready for some fun tonight? Good food and fireworks." He smiled.

Chaun felt her head nod next to his. "Yes I am. Due to the arid climate, we didn't get to have fireworks too often in Colorado. It varied from year to year."

"Well it's a rarity here that you don't get to have fireworks on the fourth." Denise let go and sat down next to Chaun.

She took a sip of her coffee. "Well, that sounds promising." Denise looked across at Sam sitting in her high chair. "It looks like she is enjoying being outside today."

Chaun laughed. "Yeah she's been happy outside. She could have got that from either one of us." He looked down and then back at Denise a moment later, his expression apologetic. "I'm sorry. I shouldn't have brought that up."

Denise placed her hand on Chaun's forearm. "It's fine. You don't have to apologize for anything. I'm not Katrina. You don't

have to worry about bringing up people from your past around me."
Chaun nodded in response.

As they were talking, Michelle had gone back into the house
to prepare some of the other side dishes for dinner. She was in the
middle of chopping an onion and singing her favorite song. The
knife stopped mid-slice, she stopped singing, and her irises turned
black all at the same instant. Her mouth eased back to form a wicked
grin. She walked over to the mirror and looked at the reflection.
"Hello Michelle. I'm going…to borrow your body for a while." The
entity laughed. Unlike the Chaplain the entity allowed Michelle to
see what was happening while she was possessed.

The entity looked down at the large knife in her hand.
"Nah… don't want to get messy this early." Michelle's head rose to
see the fireworks lying on the side table just inside the patio door.
"Perfect." They walked to the door and rummaged through the bag
of fireworks. They came across two strands of firecrackers. The
entity pulled them out and exposed the fuses on each. "Hmmm… not
long enough." It began looking through the bag. "Where are… the
fuses? I know Dave… usually keeps… extras. He always was…
safety conscious." It found a box with the fuses inside. "Ah… here

we are." The entity opened the box and broke off a length of fuse that would burn for a second or two. It added each of these to the existing fuse on the strands of firecrackers. The entity slowly slid the door open and stepped outside. The firecrackers held with fuses touching in her right hand and the lighter held in the left. It eased up behind Chaun and Denise, lit the fuses, and threw one under each person.

Dave looked up just as the firecrackers began detonating under Chaun and Denise. He noticed Michelle's eyes fade from black to her usual brown. The instant her eyes regained their normal hue, Sam began laughing a high pitched, shrieking laugh. He turned to see Sam's eyes, black, looking with pride at the scene unfolding. Denise and Chaun were screaming and hollering, and were already out of their chairs. Chaun turned to Michelle, "What the hell were you thinking mom?"

Her expression was one of complete shock. Her mouth was open and her eyes wide. Chaun's comment hit a chord causing her eyes to mist. "It wasn't me."

"Sure, it wasn't mom." His voice raising to almost a yell.

Dave spoke up, "Chaun. Don't speak to your mother like that. She's telling the truth." He turned his head and looked at Sam. "Isn't she?"

Everyone turned and looked at the entity looking at them with a smug look. "I told you things would get worse. I wasn't lying. I promise you, things will continue to get worse before they get better."

"How have I wronged you to make you do this?" Chaun said with a look of total concern.

Sam's brow raised then lowered. "If you don't know…then maybe I shouldn't restrain myself. I think…no. You will find out in due time." With this the entity left Sam and was gone for the time being.

Chaun looked at Michelle. His expression was flat except for his jaw hanging open. "I'm sorry mom. I thought you had thrown the firecrackers under us as a prank."

"It's okay honey. You should know by now that I wouldn't do such a thing. Your father on the other hand would definitely do something of that nature." Her eyes squinted. "There was something weird though."

Chaun asked, "What do you mean?" His brow furrowed.

"When I was possessed…" She paused for a moment while thinking of how to describe what had occurred. "the entity allowed me to see what was happening and hear her thoughts. She knows us."

Chaun's voice almost mocking due to his perception that Michelle was stating the obvious. "Of course, she knows us. That's why she's haunting us."

"No, I don't mean knows us as an acquaintance. She knows our habits." She raised her hand towards Dave. "She knew your father always bought fuses to attach to fireworks for safety. She knew it was a habit of his every year."

"That is odd. I don't know what to say or do, other than to give it time. It will let us know who it is when it's ready or when it dawns on us."

Chapter 20

The doorbell rang throughout the house. It was four in the afternoon. Dave walked to the door. Who the hell is here? We weren't expecting anyone. Dave opened the door to find Jake standing on the other side. He smiled wide and offered his hand. "Jake, how the hell are you?"

Jake grinned and shook Dave's hand. "I'm great Dave. How are you?"

Dave stepped to the side and gestured for Jake to enter. Jake stepped into the house. Dave closed the door then turned and placed his hand on Jake's shoulder. "Not too bad. I take it you're here to see Chaun?"

Jake smiled and gave Dave a sideways glance. "And the rest of the family. Has he been holding up all right?"

Dave pursed his lips. "As good as can be expected. Things have been a little complicated around here lately."

Jake looked at Dave curiously. "Family arguments?"

Dave smiled and let out a nervous laugh. "Actually, no. I wish it were that simple. We have a ghost that's been haunting us."

Dave and Jake walked through the house towards the doors leading to the backyard. When they stepped through the glass doors Jake saw that they had the umbrella open for shade. Everyone was sitting underneath it. "Hey everyone, figured I would stop by for a chat."

Chaun stood and shook Jake's hand. He smiled ear to ear. He then said, "Thanks for coming by, finally. I think the last time I spoke with you was in the hospital right before I was discharged."

Jake looked towards the ground. "Yeah I know. I should have at least called." He looked back up at Chaun with a sheepish smile. "Sorry man, work's been crazy lately."

Chaun laughed, reached out, and smacked Jake's upper arm. "It's okay. I'm just giving you a hard time. It is good to see you though."

"Likewise." Jake laughed slightly. "Your dad was trying to tell me you guys are being haunted. You guys don't believe in the paranormal. I should know better than to believe your dad…always trying to prank someone." Jake smiled thinking that Dave and Chaun would reveal it was all a joke.

Chaun looked at Dave with a serious expression. He looked back at Jake. He bit his upper lip in slight frustration knowing that getting Jake to believe the truth may take some time. Jake's smile changed from one of fun and games to a smile of disbelief. He looked around to see if anyone was grinning at the joke. Jake was dumbfounded to find that every single face was serious. Chaun spoke up, he motioned to the seat in front of Jake. "Please have a seat." Jake sat down next to Sam.

"You mean to tell me you guys have a ghost?" Chaun nodded. "Do you see a form moving through the house like a mist?" Chaun shook his head slowly from side to side. "What the hell does it do?"

"It moves shit from time to time…" Chaun looked down and then back up with a look that portrayed great discomfort. His eyes narrowed to a squint expecting Jake's reaction. "and possesses people."

Jake shook his head while laughing nervously. "You've got to be kidding me. I still don't believe it. Who does it possess?"

Chaun shrugged and raised his hands, palms skyward, and let them drop. "Whoever it wants. The majority of the time it possesses Sam."

The next voice Jake heard came from the highchair next to him. The voice was high pitched. The instant he heard it he felt chills so cold it would have made an ice cube sliding down his spine feel like hot wax. "Jake…" Jake turned to see Sam staring directly into his eyes. He had never seen eyes that dark. "believe it." He then watched the blackness of Sam's eyes fade as if it was mist on water being replaced by the blue of Sam's eyes. For Jake everything went black. For everyone else, they watched as Jake's head slammed into the table as he feinted. Denise rushed over and within a few minutes had Jake awake. Michelle had gone in for a damp rag.

Jake rapidly blinked as he came to and cradled his head in his hands. His head throbbed with pain. "What happened? I remember seeing Sam talking to me, then everything went black."

Dave responded, "You feinted. Do you believe us now?" Jake slowly nodded his head.

Michelle handed him a cup of water and he took a sip. "Who is it?"

Dave shook his head. "We still haven't figured that out."

Jake's brow raised and his voice grew anxious. "I'm pretty sure that would be pretty important to finding answers."

Chaun nodded his head. "I fully agree."

Chapter 21

By the middle of October, the leaves on the trees had begun to change, Sam had grown a little bigger, the air grew colder, and the entity had kept to its typical routine. Denise grew anxious about the evening that Chaun and her were about to spend together. Dave and Michelle had offered to watch Samantha while they were gone. She walked around the grocery store wondering how things would play out throughout the evening.

No matter how much she tried not to think about Chaun, he was always there. Her days were brighter when she was able to be around him or even hear his voice. She got in line at the checkout lane and slowly made her way forward. She had gotten enough to fill a hand basket. Denise had not realized that the person in line had already checked out. The cashier looked at her and said, "Ma'am? Ma'am. Ma'am!" Denise came back to reality from her daydreaming about Chaun. "Are you okay?"

She gave and apologetic grin. "Yes, I'm sorry. I'm fine."

The cashier looked at Denise without a hint of judgment in her eyes. "Is it a guy?"

Denise looked at the cashier and saw that she was smiling. She seemed to be about the same age as Denise. "Yeah. I can't stop thinking about him. Every time I try not to think about him, my mind automatically goes to nothing but him."

She grinned as she began scanning Denise's items. "Sounds like someone is in love. Have you asked him out yet?"

The cashier noticed the longing, sad, far off look in Denise's eyes. Denise shook her head. "Not yet. I'm letting him take things at his pace." The cashier gave her a skeptical look. "It's kind of complicated. His wife was killed in a car accident about a year ago. I met him while he was in the hospital. I was one of his nurses."

The cashier's eyes widened as her mouth dropped open. "Are you talking about Chaun Hutchins?"

Denise's right brow lowered. "Yes, I am. Do you know him?"

"I graduated with him. How is he?" Her face portrayed genuine concern.

Denise responded, "He's doing okay. He is living with his parents for the time being."

The cashier frowned as her face reddened. "I felt so bad when I found out what had happened. Someone like Chaun didn't deserve that kind of trial. He always was a sweetheart."

Denise smiled. "He still is." Her brow furrowed. "Did you ever meet his wife?"

Her expression grew angry and her face reddened. "Unfortunately, yes. I don't like to talk bad about the dead, but she was a real bitch. At the class reunions everyone would talk about her and agree that Chaun could do better. He hardly talked with her around. She would yell at him and demand stuff from him. From what I had seen of her, she never treated him like a person."

Denise was hurt by this news. Hearing about Chaun's poor treatment from an outside perspective made the reality that much harder to bare. "I kind of figured that from some of the behaviors I've noticed in him. He always apologizes for the smallest things. I'm just hoping I can pull him out of the mindset that she had on him."

The cashier smiled, "If I know Chaun, he'll bounce back in no time. That'll be five dollars and twenty-three cents."

Denise removed six dollars from her purse and handed it to the cashier. "Here you go hon."

The cashier handed her the change. She smiled. Her face portrayed caring and understanding. "Have a good day sweetie. Tell Chaun and his parents that Melissa says hi."

Denise returned the smile and nodded as she grabbed her bags. "Thank you. I will. Have a good day hon."

"You do the same."

Chapter 22

After Denise had been at Dave and Michelle's home for about a half an hour, a knock was heard at the door. Chaun said he would answer it. He got out of his chair and walked to the front door. He came back into the room, "Denise." She looked up at him. "You ready to go?"

"Yeah." She stood up. Chaun walked over to her and helped her with her coat. She turned to Dave and Michelle. "It was good talking with you guys."

Dave responded, as he gave her a courteous smile. "Denise, it's always a pleasure."

Denise walked to the front door. She was ecstatic when she noticed that a limousine was parked in the driveway. It was a thing of beauty. This wasn't any regular car style limousine. It was a black Lincoln Navigator. Michelle spoke from behind her and Chaun, "You guys have a great time. If you need anything call us and if something comes up here, we'll call you. Love you Chaun."

"We will. Love you to mom." With that he began walking towards the limo with his hand gently on the small of Denise's back.

She almost cried that someone would think highly enough of her to rent a limo for the evening instead of driving. They walked to the limo and the driver opened the back door for Chaun and Denise. They both climbed in and looked around when they sat down. The driver climbed in and rolled down the window separating the seating areas.

He spoke with an even tone. "There are drinks in the mini fridge. There is also a bottle of champagne that is already chilled. Where are we headed tonight? I know you've reserved my services for the duration of the evening."

Chaun smiled and spoke with a respectful light-hearted tone. "Indianapolis, please. What is your name sir?"

"Samuel, sir."

"Nice to meet you Samuel. My name is Chaun."

Samuel dipped his head respectfully. "Likewise, sir. If you need to speak with me just pick up the phone."

"Will do. Thank you, Samuel."

"You're welcome sir." Samuel turned and rolled up the window. He backed out of the driveway. They were on their way to Indianapolis. The ride to their destination was uneventful. Chaun and

Denise drank a couple glasses of Champagne and snacked on fruit. They talked the entire way down, including where they had decided to go for dinner.

Chaun told Samuel what restaurant at which they wished to dine. What he said next surprised Samuel, "When we get there, if you're hungry, I want you to feel free to go in and order something to eat. The dinner will be on me."

Samuel was awestruck at Chaun's gesture. He smiled in disbelief. "Thank you, sir. That is kind of you."

When they arrived at the restaurant for dinner, Samuel parked in front of the door, walked around and opened the door for Chaun and Denise allowing them to exit the vehicle before closing the door behind them. "Thank you, Samuel. If you want to eat, I'll let the hostess know that I'll pick up the check."

"Thank you again sir." Samuel walked back around the limousine, got in, and drove off to find a place to park.

Chaun and Denise entered the restaurant. Chaun looked at the hostess and spoke, "There will be two of us tonight. If the limo driver comes in to eat, could you please tell his waitress to put his food on my bill?"

The hostess nodded, "I can most definitely do that sir. Table or booth?"

Chaun looked at Denise. She turned to the hostess and said, "Booth, please."

The hostess turned, retrieved two menus and two rolls of silverware, and lead them to their booth. "Here you are and your waitress will be right with you."

Chaun gave a polite nod. "Thank you, ma'am." Chaun said. "You want an appetizer, or just the entrée?"

Denise opened up her menu and began to look it over. "Let's just have the entrée. We probably will want to save room for snacks at the game."

The waitress arrived at the table. She was probably in her mid-forties. "Good evening. My name's Dorothy and I will be taking care of you two this evening. Can I start by getting you something to drink?" She turned to look at Denise.

"I'll have an unsweet tea." Denise said.

"I'll have the same."

"Two unsweet teas, I'll be back with those in just a few minutes."

Chaun smiled. "Thank you, Dorothy."

"You're welcome." Dorothy walked away from the table.

Denise continued to look at her menu when she asked, "What are you having?"

Chaun tone was positive yet determined. "I'm thinking of having a steak and shrimp. What are you thinking of having?"

Denise's voice sounded distant. "I'm not sure. It all sounds so good. I may go with the grilled chicken."

"That doesn't sound like a bad choice." Chaun said. Denise looked up at him and smiled.

Dorothy returned to the table and placed their teas in front of them. "Here you are. Are you ready to order or do you need more time?"

Chaun looked at Denise and nodded. Denise looked at Dorothy and said, "I think we're ready. I'm going to have the grilled chicken breast with the steamed vegetables." Dorothy scribbled on her notepad.

Dorothy stopped writing for a second as she turned to Chaun. "I will have the steak and shrimp with a baked sweet potato."

"How would you like your steak cooked?"

162

"Medium well, please." Chaun handed the menus to Dorothy. "Thank you, ma'am." He smiled at her as she took the menus from Chaun.

She smiled and winked Chaun. "You're quite welcome. I will get these put in and bring it out when it's ready." Dorothy walked away from the table once again.

Chaun looked at Denise. "I don't know about you, but it's nice to get away from everything for a while."

She let out a sigh. "I agree. Work has been a bear lately."

Chaun shook his head and reached across the table taking Denise's hands and holding them in his own. "I can't imagine some of the issues you deal with at work. I know nursing is one of the higher stress occupations."

Denise nodded. Her expression was sullen. "That it is. There are times when it's really rewarding, and there are also times when it almost breaks you." Her eyes looked into Chaun's and her face and tone brightened. "So, what's it like not having to work?"

Chaun smiled. "There are times it drives me up the wall, but then knowing I have a clear schedule to spend time with Sam, my parents, or you is consoling." He looked down then back up at

Denise. "I think I'll be able to manage without working. Hell, if I get too bored, I can always pick up a hobby."

"You could always pick up paranormal investigations." Chaun looked at her almost angry. He stopped himself from saying anything out of anger when he saw the grin on her face. They both began laughing. He had almost forgotten how good it felt to laugh. It was one of those laughs that almost brought him to tears.

He looked down then back up at Denise. "Yeah I could. I've had enough experience with it." He paused for a moment. "What is your take on the situation?"

Denise's face straightened, as she thought of how to voice her feelings. Her voice was soft and distant. "I have no idea. Before I met you and started witnessing and experiencing the events that your family and I have, I didn't believe in ghosts or entities. I was like so many others thinking that once we were gone our souls went on to different places. I didn't think that something could be left behind." Her eyes narrowed. "What's your opinion of it? Are you handling it okay?"

Chaun leaned back in the seat. In a more serious tone he said, "I'm doing about as well as I can be. I know that whatever happens I must remain strong. As for my opinion of the situation," He leaned forward again. He spoke with a tone that portrayed disbelief. "I was pretty much in the same mindset as you. I believed that once we died, that was it, there was nothing left except our bodies."

Her face lengthened and her voice shaky. "Are you scared that the entity will follow through with what it has promised?"

Chaun looked down at his hands on the table. They were joined with interlocking fingers. He let out a sigh and spoke with a worried tone. "Yes, and it frightens me to no end. If it causes harm to anyone, I wish it would be me. I don't know who it is that's haunting us, but apparently they have a lot of anger towards me for something I have done."

Denise nodded her head, glanced down at Chaun's hands, then back up at him. "Who have you wronged to make them want to hurt you?"

Chauns brow raised and he shook his head. "I don't know, and it's bugging the hell out of me."

Denise just nodded in response. She was quiet for a moment. Due to her anticipation her voice became livelier. "On a lighter note, I'm anxious to see the game tonight. It's been so long since I've been to an actual hockey game. I catch them all the time on T.V., but seeing a game live is so much more exciting."

Chaun grinned. "I could not agree more. When you see a game live, there are things you can't really fathom just seeing it on the T.V. screen. The smell of the ice and the roaring energy of the crowd are two of the things I look forward to when attending a live game."

Denise sat up in the booth a little bit and her smile widened. "Especially when a fight breaks out."

Chaun took a drink from his glass and dipped his head as he set the glass down. "Oh, that's always a given. I've been meaning to ask you for some time, what are some of the other things you enjoy?"

Her smile narrowed in contemplation, "I'm trying to think of something I have not yet told you. I love to read."

Chaun's lips pursed. "What genre do you like to read? Do you read simply for surface meaning or analytically?"

She took a drink. "I like romance from time to time, but you can never go wrong with the classics. Twain, Faulkner, and Poe are just a few. I love reading stories for the story itself, but I also enjoy reading analytically."

"That's cool. I love reading as well, and like you, I love to read both for story and underlying meanings."

Denise's smile faded to a look of concern. "Can I ask you a question? If you don't feel like answering it's okay, I'll understand if you don't want to answer."

Chaun looked into her eyes and his tone was gentle yet serious. "You can feel free to ask me any question you like."

Denise nodded, looked down, and then spoke in a hesitant tone. "What was Katrina like? I know that things were difficult from what you told me while you were in the hospital."

Chaun's brow furrowed portraying his attempt at finding the best way to express his answer truthfully. "What all did I tell you?"

Her eyes looked to her right. "She always had to be the center of attention and have her way, with no regard of how it affected others."

Chaun grabbed his glass, set it between both hands, and fidgeted with it as he spoke. "She had moments where she could be a total sweetheart. Unfortunately, most of the time she was demanding

167

and mean. It didn't matter who she had to talk down to as long as she got her way. That's all that mattered to her."

"Including you." Denise stated.

Chaun gave a slight nod. "Which, always put me at the top of the list. It always seemed like I could not do right by her. Everything I did was wrong. There were times, while we were out in public, I could read in people's eyes that they were awestruck that I was with her. Their eyes would plead with me to leave her."

She reached out and placed her hands on either side of his. Her tone soft and pure. "It almost sounds like she was verbally abusive." Chaun paused for a couple seconds after hearing this from Denise. "If you think I'm in the wrong, please say so."

His eyes were wide with the realization that she was right. "No, actually I believe you are dead on. I never realized it before, but I believe you're right. That would be the only explanation for some of the behavioral side effects of my relationship with her. Like me apologizing on the fourth for mentioning her."

Denise frowned. "I'm sorry you had to experience that type of treatment. No one should be treated like shit, especially by the person that is supposed to make you whole. You should have been able to find support and gain confidence from her, not lose confidence and have no emotional support."

Chaun gave a pained grin. "There was actually a time, earlier in our relationship that, an uncle of mine passed. I was deeply saddened by his passing. She told me to get over it and that it happens."

Her head lowered. "Was this after the funeral?"

Chaun shook his head as Denise looked back up at him. "No, this was the day of or the day after his passing. We hadn't even had the funeral yet."

Chaun saw the hurt in Denise's eyes. She looked as if she was about to start crying. "I'm truly sorry Chaun. You deserve better. I hope you do find happiness, true happiness and not false hopes."

He looked down at their hands. Chaun moved his hands away from the glass, turned them over to grasp hers, then moved them to the center of the table. He looked into her eyes. "The difference between you and Katrina seems like night and day. Thank you for showing me that there are people in the world that can be heartfelt and genuine."

She smiled, "I'm just being myself."

There was a caring sternness in his voice. "And that's all you ever should be, nothing more and nothing less." Dorothy arrived with their food.

Dorothy said, "Here you go, steak and shrimp, and the grilled chicken. Do you guys need anything else?"

Chaun shook his head and smiled at Dorothy. "No ma'am not at the moment. Thank you so much."

She smiled as she placed extra napkins on the table. "You're very welcome hon, if you need anything you just let me know."

Chaun and Denise enjoyed their dinner together. The conversation was lighter throughout their meal. Both of them shared jokes and stories they had heard. When Dorothy brought out the check, Chaun was pleased to see that an order had been placed at the bar for a dinner to go. He paid the bill. The two then walked out the door to find the limo waiting on them with Samuel holding the door open.

Denise got into the limousine first. Chaun dipped his head at Samuel. "Thank you, Samuel. Did you enjoy your dinner?" Chaun asked.

Samuel shook Chaun's hand. "Very much sir. Thank you. Not many people are kind enough to purchase a dinner for me."

"You're very welcome." Chaun climbed into the limo and Samuel closed the door behind him.

A minute later Samuel climbed into the front seat and asked, "Where to sir?"

"We are actually going to see a hockey game from here. Do you know where the venue is located?"

Samuel smiled and winked. "That I do sir, I am a hockey fan myself."

Chaun dipped his head, then grinned mischievously. "Good. In that case, you are catching the game tonight."

Samuel's jaw dropped. "Thank you, sir." Samuel turned and drove away from the restaurant en route to the rink.

Chapter 23

As they pulled to the front of the venue, Chaun was surprised to find that the lines were not long. Usually, the few times he had been there, the place was packed. Today was different. Samuel pulled to the curb and did a limo driver's normal routine. As Chaun and Denise stepped out of the limo Chaun looked at Samuel and said, "Wait here a moment."

Samuel dipped his head. "Will do, sir."

Chaun walked through the door with his arm around Denise's waist. Her hand was on his shoulder. He stepped up to the ticket counter and asked for three tickets, two together and one near an exit. He paid for the tickets and walked back out to Samuel. He handed him the ticket for the seat that was close to an exit. "Here you are Samuel. I made sure it was by an exit. I figured if you needed to step out early to make sure the limousine was at the curb it would give you an easy exit."

Samuel's grin stretched from ear to ear. His voice ecstatic as he dipped his head a few times. "Thank you so much sir. It has been a really long time since I've seen a game in person."

Chaun shook Samuel's hand. "You're very welcome Samuel. Enjoy the game."

Samuel said almost shouting. "You do the same sir. I will have the limo pulled up to this very spot by the time you walk out of those doors."

"Thank you, Samuel." Chaun and Denise turned to enter through the doors once more. After handing the staff member at the door their tickets and entering, they headed for the skate shop. Looking at Denise and smiling Chaun said, "You want a hockey jersey?"

Her brow lowered on the left side of her face. "You serious?"

"Yep, take your pick." He smiled when Denise's face lit up. Denise grabbed a jersey that she liked. Chaun grabbed one as well. He also picked up a few things for Samantha while he was there. While walking the corridor, they tore the tags off of their jerseys and put them on. They stopped at a vendor between the shop and their seating area. As they stood in line Chaun looked at Denise and asked, "What are you getting?"

She looked reluctant. "I'm actually still kind of full from dinner. At the least, I will get a beer."

"Actually, a beer does sound really good. I may get a bratwurst as well, can't break tradition." He smiled at her.

She grinned. "Well in that case I better order one as well. Don't want to break tradition, as well as bring bad luck." Chaun gave a slight laugh in response.

After Chaun purchased the Brats and Beer, they topped them however they saw fit and went to find their seats. Denise was surprised to find that the seats were near the ice, but far enough back to where the glass didn't hinder being able to see the rink in its entirety. The game had not even started yet and Chaun and Denise could tell the energy was already high. Within a few minutes of sitting down the lights dimmed and the rink lit up with spotlights and strobe lights as the players were announced. After both teams had been announced, the American and Canadian national anthems were played. Everyone stood for the national anthem and then sat back down.

The game was a close and exciting one. Four players were ejected during the second period when a huge fight broke out. After stepping between two players, a referee was knocked on his ass due to getting punched the face. The game was tied at the end of three periods, went into overtime, and then continued on into a shootout after neither team scored in overtime. Chaun and Denise walked away from their seats with their throats almost raw from screaming and cheering so much during the game.

As promised, Samuel was waiting on the curb when they exited the building. When they approached the limo, Samuel opened the door. Chaun was all smiles when he asked, "Did you watch the game?"

Samuel grinned and said, "I did sir. Thank you. I haven't seen a game that exciting in quite some time."

Chaun gave a quick nod. "You are very welcome." Chaun entered the limo. After he heard Samuel get into the limo, he picked up the phone.

Samuel picked up the receiver located on the console next to the driver's seat. "Yes sir?"

"Samuel, I want you to know I'm calling the company tomorrow." Chaun hung the receiver up and moved to the seat on the opposite side of the glass from Samuel. He lightly knocked on the glass. A second later Samuel rolled the glass down between the seating areas. Chaun could tell Samuel was very worried that he had done something wrong. "I want you to know you are not in trouble for anything. I have been testing you tonight. The reason for my calling the company tomorrow is not to complain. You have been very hospitable tonight." Chaun paused for a couple seconds. When he spoke next he looked directly into Samuel's eyes. "I am calling the company to let them know you are an exceptional driver. I will be asking them to keep you available if I need to hire the company's services. I want you to be my driver if I take any more trips out of my local area." Chaun could see Samuel's expression change from a furrowed look of worry to a joyful smile which portrayed gratitude. Chaun smiled at the change.

"Thank you sir. That means a lot." Samuel laughed. "You had me terrified for a couple moments there."

Chaun jokingly grimaced. "Sorry for that. I meant what I said though, you are very, very good at your job. Don't ever let that change."

Samuel shook his head. "I won't sir. Where would you like to go?"

"I think we are about ready to head north. I'm sure you've got to be fairly tired." His eyes lowered then rose to meet Samuel's again. "Are you a big coffee drinker?"

"Tired… yes. As for coffee, I love it." Samuel grinned.

Chaun smiled. "Good, if you want to drive through a coffee shop before heading north. All of us can order a drink. I'm sure I want to stay awake for a while."

Samuel smiled in return. "That sounds like a wonderful plan sir." Chaun returned to his seat next to Denise, Samuel rolled the window back up, and pulled away from the curb. They drove through the drive-thru at the coffee shop. Chaun paid for the entire order. As they headed back home Chaun and Denise talked about the game and the evening.

Chapter 24

As the limo pulled into the drive at Dave and Michelle's house, both Chaun and Denise were surprised at how alert they were. Samuel parked, got out and opened the door for the two. When Chaun got out of the car he looked at Samuel. The two shook hands, then Samuel turned to Denise, shook her hand, and gave a shallow bow. "Thank you again for being so professional and personable tonight. I will call the company tomorrow and see about what we had discussed, unless you are not okay with it."

Samuel shook his head almost frantically. "No sir. I am more than okay with it. You have treated me better than anyone I've worked for in all my years working in this field. Thank you again for the compliment."

Chaun dipped his head. "I was only speaking the truth. Have a good evening Samuel and drive safe."

Samuel dipped his head respectfully to Chaun and closed the door to the Limo. "I will and you have a good night as well sir." Samuel smiled, got in the limousine, and backed out of the driveway.

Chaun and Denise slowly walked towards the front door. Luckily, his parents were thoughtful enough to leave the porch light on so they did not trip walking up the stairs to the front porch. He unlocked and opened the door being as quiet as possible, trying not to wake his parents or Sam. When they got inside, Chaun helped Denise out of her coat and hung it up in the closet. After hanging up the coats he came back to find that she was in the kitchen getting a glass of water. She sat down at the island while she slowly sipped at her drink. "Do you want to stay up and chat more?"

Chaun walked to the opposite side of the island and leaned against it. "Might not be a bad idea. How tired are you?"

She propped her elbow on the island and rested her head on her hand. "Not too tired. I could definitely stay up and talk to you longer."

Denise smiled, "Good. We will definitely have to do this again. I had such a blast tonight. Thank you for taking me."

Chaun blushed. "You're more than welcome."

"That was really nice of you to treat Samuel tonight. He seems like a sweet man."

Chaun nodded as Denise took another drink of water. "Yes he does. I just figured, he probably is ignored and taken for granted most of the time. I am blessed to have so much. I just wanted to give some back where I could."

She looked into his eyes. "You know Chaun, you're not like most other guys. Most of them would have just let him sit in the car." Her voice grew reflective. It also sounded like she pitied Samuel. She looked down at the glass in her hand. "Hell, most of the time, he probably packs a lunch to eat while his passengers are inside."

Chaun dipped and tilted his head simultaneously. "More than likely, and that's why I treated him tonight. I know you're not tired yet, but would you be up for a movie in my room? At least until we get tired?"

Denise took another sip of water before she spoke. "Sure. What movie did you have in mind?"

Chaun crossed his arms, rested his arms on the island, and set his chin on his forearm. "I figured I'd leave that choice up to you. Are you in the mood for a comedy, action, romance, horror? The choices are endless."

She smiled. "What about an action flick? I'd say a horror movie, but I tend to scream pretty loud while watching those." I'm pretty sure we're not wanting to wake Sam or your parents.

"That sounds like a plan." Chaun said. Denise stood up, slid her stool back up to the island, walked to the sink, dumped the remaining contents of her glass, and placed it in the dishwasher.

She had a mischievous grin on her face when she turned. "I want to do something tonight and am wondering if you will be okay with it."

Chaun's eyes narrowed as he leaned his head back slightly. "I thought you said you weren't going to force the issue."

Denise smiled. "Who said it had to do with sex? Hmmm…someone has their mind in the gutter." She laughed when she saw Chaun blush slightly. "Actually, Mr. Hutchins, I was going to ask if I could wear your hockey jersey as a nightie."

Chaun grinned. "I wouldn't mind that at all." He wrapped his arm around her waist as they ascended the stairs. Chaun stopped at the top of the stairs and walked into the nursery to check on Sam before they went to his room which was at the end of the hall. He walked in to find that Sam was sleeping soundly. Dave and Michelle would brag about how good of a baby she was within the first few months. While he was in the hospital, they would always say that she hardly ever cried, and that she laughed most of the time. Chaun smiled slightly at the appreciation of her being a blessing in his life. He turned to find that Denise was leaning her head and one hand on the door frame with the rest of her body out in the hallway. From the smile on her face he could tell that she loved him deeply.

They left the nursery and walked down the hall to his room. As they entered Chaun walked around to the T.V. located in the far corner of his room. He chose an action movie and placed the DVD in the player. During the lag between the startup and the disc menu, Chaun took off his jersey and laid it on the bed. He then stripped down to his boxer briefs.

Denise stood by his closet. She was waiting for him to get undressed before undressing. She grabbed Chaun's jersey off of the bed. Since that first night of her sleeping in bed with Chaun, he had always looked away as she undressed and put on a night shirt. She looked at him, after grabbing the jersey, "No peaking." She smiled. He turned his head away as Denise turned facing the closet. She had stripped down to her bra and underwear before sneaking a glance to see if his head was still turned. She was surprised to find him staring at her grinning. "I thought I told you no peaking? If you stare too hard, you'll go cross eyed."

He held up his hands and smiled. "I'm sorry. I couldn't help myself."

She smiled and turned back to face the closet. She unhooked her bra, removed it, and put on Chaun's jersey. She turned back around to find that Chaun had climbed into bed and pulled back the covers on her side of the bed. She climbed in and pulled the covers up. Chaun hit play on the controller to start the DVD.

Denise snuggled up to his chest as the movie started. Chaun's mind raced with his feelings for Denise. Over the last few months he had realized that at some point his feelings had gone from like to love. That night had been so perfect. She was so heartfelt and genuine. No one had ever treated him with the care and kindness she always had shown him. He cherished her. As the opening credits flashed across the screen, he said to her, his expression was one of pain and concern, "Denise, I want to tell you something."

She sat up. When she saw the look on his face, she grew worried. She rested her head against the headboard. "Is everything okay?"

He gave her a soft reassuring smile. "Yeah, I want you to know, I cherish you and your company. I love you Denise. I love the person you are and the person you've always been to me. I think I'm ready to take that step past friendship." Even in the glow of the T.V. he could tell she was beaming.

A tear fell from her left eye and glistened in the light. "I love you to." Chaun leaned over and kissed her. He slid down onto his back from a seated position. Denise lay next to him kissing him. He caressed her cheek and neck with his right hand. His left hand he slid under Denise's hip. He lifted her hip silently telling her to change position. Denise straddled him and continued kissing him. He began lifting at the hem of the jersey. She grabbed the bottom of the jersey about ready to pull it off.

Chaun then noticed that he could see her breath as a mist. It can't be that cold in here. Denise's head snapped back and she began screaming. Chaun noticed that her hair was pulled straight back. It looked as if an invisible fist had grasped a chunk of Denise's hair and held her head back. Chaun was paralyzed as Denise was lifted into the air by her hair. Her feet dangled a foot above his legs. Her breath clouded in faster repetition with each passing second. Her body was then thrown against the wall above his headboard. Denise's head slammed repeatedly into the wall above his bed.

After her head connected with the wall the second time, Chaun heard footsteps running down the hall and his parents yelling. Denise was thrown across the room with enough force the drywall was damaged. A void was left not only where she contacted the wall opposite his bed, but above his bed as well. Chaun quickly sat up in bed. He stared at Denise's body lying in a heap on the floor. As the door opened and Dave and Michelle entered, his face was forcefully turned towards them.

Dave immediately ran towards Denise. His tone anxious and worried. "What the hell happened?" Chaun stared blankly. "Chaun!" Chaun looked Dave in the eye. "Oh my God." Dave pointed at Chaun. "Michelle, get two compresses. What happened?" Michelle left the room to get damp towels from the bathroom.

Chaun sat, eyes distant. "I don't know. Things were getting hot."

Dave's brow furrowed. His voice stern. "And it led to this? How?"

Chaun finally looked at Dave, but his look was still distant. He shook his head. "I don't know. She was straddling me, and then was lifted into the air. She was thrown into the wall above my bed, her head was slammed into the wall, and then she was thrown across the room."

Dave froze with his mouth agape. He turned to Denise. "Denise. Denise. Can you hear me sweetie?" She let out a slight moan. "Oh, thank God, she's alive."

She became more alert. She reached up and grabbed her head. Her voice was groggy. "What happened and how did I get on the floor?"

Dave looked at her. His voice was soft as he shook his head. Michelle came back in the room with the compresses. "We don't know. Chaun said you had your head slammed into the wall and were thrown across the room."

What they heard next made each of them feel like a drop of liquid nitrogen had run down their spine. A high-pitched laugh emanated loudly from the nursery. Chaun took the compress from

Michelle and held pressure to his face. She handed the other compress to Denise. He got out of bed and helped Dave assist Denise to her feet. All four of them went as a group to the next room. What they saw when they entered the room paralyzed each of them in place. Sam sat on the side of her crib with her feet laced between the bars for stability. Her eyes were blacker than usual in the darkness. The laugh was coming from her.

Something on the wall alerted Chaun. He turned to see something written on the wall. Chaun reached over and flipped the light switch to reveal the words, "My lust for revenge is not satiated yet."

Chaun looked at Sam. His voice oozed anger and frustration, and his face redder than the crimson blood seeping from it. "What do you want?"

Sam's face changed from a menacing grin to a flat expression. The change was so fast it seemed as if a switch had been flipped. Her tone was low, but mean. "I told you. I want you… to suffer." Turning to Denise the entity said, her voice smug. "How's the head feeling? I bet you have… one hell of a headache. I would too… after that ass kicking." It looked back at Chaun, "There is…

still more to come. Could be less severe, could be more. It just depends… on my mood." The entity carefully maneuvered back down into the crib. It sat down. The pupils once again inhaled the dissipating blackness. Chaun's blood dripped from his chin and splattered on the floor. The sound of his dripping blood and the labored breathing from the four echoed throughout the room.

Chapter 25

It was late. Dave sat up, eyes bloodshot, staring at his computer screen. He looked at the bottom right corner, 2:30 am. He had been researching paranormal investigators. Not just to see what kind of groups were in the area, but if they even existed. The family needed help and he was open for almost any solution.

He had come across quite a few group sites that seemed promising. Dave was growing frustrated, most of the groups told him, when he phoned, that they could not make it for a couple weeks or months. He had not found anything that had looked promising for hours. He was just about to give up his search when he came across a group's website that said they were located in the neighboring county. Dave picked up the phone to call. With the phone in hand, he looked at the clock again and decided against calling that night. He would call first thing in the morning.

After drinking a glass of water, he climbed the stairs and crawled into bed. Michelle woke at his stirring. "Any luck hon?"

He nodded his head even though Michelle was facing away from him. "I found a group that's located in Cass County. I was

189

going to call, but figured it was too late. I'll call first thing in the morning after I get some sleep. Night sweetie, love you." He kissed Michelle on the forehead.

"Goodnight Dave, I love you to."

#

Alex woke, as usual, around seven o'clock in the morning. He finished his morning routine and walked into the kitchen to make a pot of coffee. He owned a small used car lot in Logansport Indiana. Most used car salesmen were known to be pushy and did not care about quality. Alex always put the customer's needs and wants first. He had all his vehicles thoroughly inspected and fixed before putting them on the lot. If a vehicle would cost more to fix than what he could sell it for, he would send it to auction or the scrap yard.

The phone rang. He lifted it out of its cradle, and looked at the caller ID. It was a number he did not recognize. He answered it. "Hi, this is Alex."

The voice was confident and polite. "Hi Alex. My name is David Hutchins. Is this the correct number for the Cass Paranormal Investigation Company?"

Alex turned and leaned back against the counter. "Yes, it is."

"I'm sorry for calling so early in the morning. My family is in dire need of help."

"It's quite alright Mr. Hutchins." Alex removed the coffee pot from the burner and poured a cup. "What are some of the problems you've been experiencing and how long have the occurrences been going on?"

"We have been experiencing issues since about February. The events have ranged from items being moved from one location to another to my son's girlfriend being attacked."

Alex's brow furrowed. "What do you mean by attacked?"

Dave's voice quieted, as if he was unsure that what he was about to say would be construed as either fact or fiction. "She was lifted into the air, thrown into walls, and had her head was slammed repeatedly into the wall above my son's bed." Alex paused before taking a sip of coffee. "Are you still there Alex?"

Alex set his cup on the counter. "Yes sir. Have you seen any apparitions?"

Dave's voice sounding sure once again. "No we haven't."

Alex thought for a few seconds. He tried to think of the right questions to ask. He needed to know the severity of the situation. "Has the entity possessed anyone?"

Dave's pause concerned Alex. He knew what the answer was going to be. "Yes, on numerous occasions."

Alex walked over to a small nook that had been remodeled into a miniature office space. He pulled out a legal pad and pen. Alex began taking notes over what Dave was telling him. "Who has the entity possessed?"

"My wife..." Dave acted like he did not want to finish the statement. His voice grew quiet. "...and my grand-daughter."

"How old is your grand-daughter?"

"Less than a year old."

Alex froze. He was speechless. In all the years he had been investigating the paranormal, he had never heard of anything like this happening. His mind raced. "Mr. Hutchins, is this a good number to reach you?"

"Yes, this is my home number."

Alex's voice grew anxious. "Good. I will call you back within the next hour or two. I'm going to call the rest of my team

192

and see what we can work out with everyone's schedules. What is the earliest you want us there?"

Dave's voice sounded worried and excited at the same time. "The sooner the better. The entity has promised that things would get worse. It has made good on that promise numerous times."

"Okay." Alex began writing again. He then wrote the names of his team members so he could make notes on who could make it to the investigation. "Even if the entire team can't make it, I'll see if I can get a couple people together to help you with the situation. I can't promise we'll catch any activity. It's usually hit and miss, but we can see what we find and give you advice on recording phenomena."

"Thank you so much Alex. I will be awaiting your call."

"You're welcome Mr. Hutchins." Alex hung up the phone. He walked down the hall and back into his bedroom. His wife was still asleep. He knelt down next to the bed. He placed his hand on her shoulder and began gently shaking her. His voice laced in urgency. "Sara. I need you to get up."

She sat up slowly. She looked at him through squinted eyes. Her tone was slightly agitated. "Why? What's up?"

"I just got a call for an investigation."

She rubbed her eyes and her tone sounded more understanding. "If you're waking me up it must be serious. How bad is it? Apparitions?"

"No. No apparitions. Some people have been possessed."

She rubbed her eyes. "Who has it possessed?"

"His wife and his grand-daughter who is less than a year old."

Her mouth fell open. "When did you tell him we'd be out?" She was already getting out of bed to start helping get things going.

"I told him I would call him back in an hour. I figured that would be enough time to contact the team, and to see what everyone's schedules were like over the next few days to a week. I've got coffee brewed in the kitchen if you want a cup."

"Thanks. I'll get my cell phone. We can start calling people." Alex turned and headed for the kitchen.

#

An hour later the phone rang in Dave's office. "Hello, this is Dave."

"Hi Dave, this is Alex. Will two nights from tonight be a good time for my team to come out?"

Dave sighed a sigh of relief. "That would be just fine. Thank you so much. All the other teams I contacted said it would be two weeks to a month before they could make it out."

"You're very welcome." His voice became hesitant. "Only three of us will be able to show up. Will that be okay?"

"That will be just fine. If you need my family to help in the investigation, we would be more than happy too."

Alex nodded and his tone was accepting. "It may not be a bad idea, especially if the haunting is directed at any person in particular. Would you be able to send me your address in an e-mail? That way I can look up directions to your house."

Dave's voice was softer and grateful. "I could do that. Thank you again Alex."

Projecting understanding and politeness, Alex said, "You're welcome Mr. Hutchins."

Dave pushed the end button on the phone, set it back in its cradle to let it charge, stood up, and walked to the kitchen. He entered to see Michelle sitting at the island, reading her book, and drinking coffee. "Morning."

She looked up, "Morning. How'd you sleep?"

He walked to the cupboard and retrieved a coffee cup. "Pretty good actually. I only got four hours of sleep, but I slept deeply." He poured his coffee into the cup.

Michelle looked up from her book. "Why so late?"

Dave turned to face her and leaned against the counter. He sipped his coffee. "I was researching paranormal investigation teams in the area."

She shot him a cynical look. "They actually have those?"

Dave laughed, "Yeah, they actually do exist. I just talked with a guy in Logansport that runs a group. He said they can be here the day after tomorrow."

"So soon?"

Dave looked down at the cup in his hand. "I told him about everything we've experienced. He got off the phone with me, contacted his team, and got back to me an hour later."

Michelle's jaw dropped. She laid her book on the island. "Was he that anxious to work with us? How much do they charge?"

196

"It's free. His insistence to help us heightened when I told him Sam was being possessed. He did ask if we would be willing to help with the investigation."

She picked up her coffee cup and took a sip. "And you told him we'd help?"

He nodded, "Yes I did. He said that the activity could be directed at one person, and having that person present could influence activity to occur."

Her brow furrowed as she set her cup down. "You didn't tell him about Chaun?"

Dave shook his head and looked at the cup in his hand once again. "No. I figured we could tell them when they get here."

"Do you even think Chaun will agree to go along with it?"

"Go along with what?" Dave and Michelle jumped at the sound of Chaun's voice. They both looked up at Chaun standing in the entryway to the kitchen.

Dave answered, "I just got off the phone with the lead person of a paranormal investigative team in Logansport."

Chaun shot Dave the same cynical look as Michelle. "They have those?"

Dave and Michelle laughed. "Yeah, they exist."

"And you're wondering if I would agree to them investigating our situation?"

Dave nodded. "That's part of it. The other part is if you'd be willing to either be present or help in the investigation."

"Do they think it will help?"

Dave sipped his coffee. "Alex, the guy I spoke with, believes so. I didn't tell him the activity was directed at you. He said if the entity was focused on one individual that having them present or helping with the investigation could prompt activity."

"If it will stop this fuck storm of a situation from continuing, I'll try anything." Dave and Michelle let Chaun's phrasing slide. On normal occasions they would have called him on it. Both understood how stressed and frustrated the last few months had made him. He walked to the far side of Dave and grabbed two coffee cups from the cabinet. He mixed sweetener, creamer, and coffee in both. "I'm going to go wake Denise." He walked toward the entryway. He stopped at the entryway. "When are they coming?"

"Day after tomorrow." Chaun nodded, stepped into the foyer, turned, and walked toward the living room.

Chapter 26

Dave, Michelle, Chaun, and Denise sat in the living room. Denise and Chaun read. Dave and Michelle were watching T.V. Chauns parents had noticed how Denise and Chaun had not even held hands since the night of the attack. They could tell both longed to show affection for each other. Due to the risk, they had decided to be safe so as not to cause more outbursts.

The identity of the entity tormenting the family was still a mystery. A few of them had speculations. Without evidence or asking the entity, they could not know concretely if their speculations were correct. The family had agreed the less amount of contact they had with the ghost the better.

The words Chaun was reading became increasingly blurry. He moved his bookmark to the open pages and closed the book. He stood up. "Well, my eyes are telling me it's time for bed." He walked to the staircase and paused.

Dave and Michelle said, "Goodnight, love you."

Chaun said, "Love you to." He looked at Denise. "Goodnight Denise." His eyes screamed the longing he felt. He wanted more than anything, to have physical contact with her again. He would even be happy with holding hands again, but he could not risk her safety.

Denise said, "Goodnight Chaun." Her look mirrored Chaun's yearning. Dave and Michelle looked at each other. Dave could tell that Michelle was on the verge of tears. They heard Chaun's footsteps ascending the stairs. When they looked back, Denise had tears rolling down her cheeks. Michelle turned off the television, walked over, and embraced Denise. Her quiet cries turned into muffled sobs. When she brought her head away from Michelle's shoulder, she noticed that Michelle was crying as well. "I'm sorry. This is ridiculous. I don't know why I'm crying so hard."

Michelle moved the hair in front of Denise's face and tucked it behind her ear. Her voice caring and soft. "Yes, you do. It's because you love him and can't show him affection."

Denise nodded.

Upstairs Chaun was struggling with the same emotions. He embraced one of the pillows Denise usually used. Over the past few nights, he had noticed that cradling one of her pillows helped him sleep a little better. He still woke up periodically, but not as much as he did the first night after the attack. Denise had suffered a concussion the night of the attack. She ended up with seven stitches in her forehead. Chaun's face did not need stitches, but it still pained him.

He was so angry and frustrated at the situation. The feeling of helplessness was overwhelming. Chaun was anxious to have the team come in so they could possibly get some of their questions answered. He was tired of not knowing. He was asleep within the next few minutes.

He dreamt of being in a graveyard. It was night and the moon was not at full, but gave enough light to illuminate details of his surroundings. Chaun stood facing Katrina's headstone. There was a cold wind blowing. The sound of dead leaves rustling in the breeze caressed his ear. He felt the pangs of sorrow and regret constrict around his heart like a belt of spikes. "Katrina, I'm sorry."

A familiar voice spoke in a derisive tone. "No, you're not." Chaun looked up behind the headstone. Katrina slowly walked towards him out of the shadows. She approached and stood behind her headstone leaning against it. "I honestly don't think you were ever sorry. You got what you wanted."

Chaun shook his head in disbelief. "What are you talking about?"

She stood up, walked around to the same side of her headstone where Chaun was standing, and sat on top of the marker with her feet hanging inches above the ground. She fidgeted with dirt that had accumulated on top of the headstone. "You are rid of me. That's basically what you said that night wasn't it?"

Chaun tilted his head down and left. His voice truthful, yet apologetic. "Some of what I said that night was the truth, but a good portion of it was spoken in anger."

Kat disappeared before his eyes. Something grabbed the hair on the back of his head. The invisible force dragged him forward and slammed his forehead into the headstone. Dazed, he fell to his knees. Katrina's torso exploded out of the ground beneath him. Her hands gripped Chaun's neck like a vice. He could barely breathe. The hair on the back of his neck stood on end and hypothermic chills ran down his spine as he looked into her eyes. They were the same black irises that had haunted the family since he came home from the hospital. Her voice thundered that high-pitched voice that usually accompanied those dreadful eyes, "You haven't suffered enough!"

Chaun's eyes opened to realize he was staring at his ceiling in a cold sweat. He threw the covers off and ran out of his room and down the stairs. He had not realized that he was in his boxer briefs. They were soaked. He reached the bottom of the stairs and came into view of Dave, Michelle, and Denise who had moved to the kitchen and were sipping on coffee. He rushed into the kitchen. Denise ran to him worried. She felt his forehead to see if he was feverish. "Chaun, what's wrong? Are you okay?"

He was pallid. His voice and breath were shaky. "Yes. Our problem just got worse. I know who's been haunting us." He paused, realizing the air seemed thick and heavy. "It's Kat."

Dave's voice was stern. "Do you know for sure?"

Chaun nodded and his voice lowered. "I think she just spoke to me in my dream."

Michelle then noticed bruising around Chaun's throat. She ran over to him for a closer inspection. "Chaun, what happened to your throat?"

Chaun ran to the entryway and looked at his reflection in the mirror. He slowly walked back to the doorway to the kitchen. "Well, that's all the evidence I need. Kat is the one haunting us."

Dave repeated his former question while looking into Chaun's eyes. "Are you sure?" Dave said in almost a whisper.

"Yeah. Mom, can you pour me a cup of coffee." Before getting his coffee, Michelle brought a quilt in from the living room and placed it on his shoulders. Chaun sat down and began telling everyone what had happened in his dream. By the time he finished everyone was staring at him with their mouths open. Chaun looked at Denise. "I'm sorry I brought this on you."

She placed her hand on top of his. "It's okay. You didn't know that your ex had been tormenting you all this time. We will get through this."

Dave said, "I will call Alex first thing in the morning and let him know." Dave and Chaun made eye contact. "Are you still willing to help with the investigation? Even with this new information?"

Chaun nodded. "I still stand behind what I said. If it will help get this entire shit storm calmed down, I'm willing to do whatever it takes. She tried to control my life while living. I sure as hell won't let her control it from the grave."

Chapter 27

The next morning Dave sat in his office. He had woke, made his coffee, and now stared at the steaming cup sitting on his desk. Chaun's news to the family the night before had raised Dave's disappointment in himself. The signs were there. He just had not put all the clues together. The three items left on the entertainment center, the entity alerting Michelle and he that something had been wrong the night Sam quit breathing, the entity's anger toward Chaun, and its hatred of Denise. It all made sense.

The number for Alex's dealership lingered on the computer screen. It was nine o'clock in the morning. Alex should be in his office by now. Dave picked up the phone and dialed the number. The phone rang on the other end. A lady with a soft voice answered, "Brinn's used cars. How may I direct your call?"

With his typical polite and kind voice he said, "Good morning ma'am. Is Alex available?"

The woman's voice grew less automated and more personable. "Yes, he is. May I ask who is calling?"

"David Hutchins."

"Just one moment Mr. Hutchins."

"Thank you."

A minute later, Alex picked up the phone. His voice sounded worried. He knew Dave would not contact him at work unless it was urgent. "Good morning Dave. Is everything all right?"

Dave said in a calm voice. "Yes," He paused for a moment. "but we've found something out that may be helpful for your investigation."

"I'm all ears Mr. Hutchins." By Dave's pause on the other end, Alex could tell that something was troubling Dave.

Knowing that what he was going to say would change the course of the investigation, Dave's voice was almost a whisper. "Chaun's wife, Katrina, is the one that's been haunting the family all this time. I told Chaun there may be a big possibility that you are going to want him to help with the investigation."

Alex nodded. "We may. Has most of the activity been directed towards him?"

Dave tapped his fingers on his desk. "Yes, most of the time when Katrina possesses Sam, she tells Chaun that he will suffer.

When Denise was physically attacked the other night it was while Chaun was making out with her."

"Hmm…did this news help with understanding the items that had been moved?"

"Yes, it did. I also have video footage of the three items being moved." Dave said with a sheepish tone. "Sorry I didn't mention it earlier. I was really tired and stressed the last time we spoke."

"We will check it out tomorrow night when we arrive. If anything else changes, feel free to give me a call."

"I will." His voice became more upbeat. "If you and the team are open to the idea, Michelle and I were thinking of cooking your team a dinner before you get started on the investigation."

Alex's smile could be heard in his voice. "That is very generous of you. My team and I will be glad to join your family for dinner. Actually it may help in gathering information for the investigation. Have a good day Mr. Hutchins. I will see you tomorrow."

"Same to you Alex and thanks again."

Alex dipped his head. "You're very welcome. Goodbye."

Dave hung up the phone and sipped his coffee.

#

Dinner had almost finished cooking by the time Alex and the team pulled into the driveway. Dave stepped out onto the front porch. The van came to a stop when parallel with the porch steps. After getting out of the vehicle, a man walked around the van from the driver's side. He looked to be in his mid-thirties. The passenger emerged from the vehicle. She appeared to be around the same age as the driver. Her hair was short and red. A third person, who appeared to be mid-twenties, stepped from the back of the van. The driver stepped up onto the porch. "David Hutchins?"

Dave dipped his head and smiled. "That I am. You must be Alex." Dave offered his hand to Alex.

Alex shook Dave's hand, and mirrored his smile. "Nice to meet you." He motioned for the woman that was with him. "This is my wife Sara." Sara shook Dave's hand. "And the other member of our team that was able to show up today is Gene." Gene dipped his head and Dave returned a nod.

Dave said, "It's a pleasure to meet all of you. Dinner has just finished cooking. Thank you again for coming."

Alex's tone was soft and understanding. "You are very welcome Mr. Hutchins."

Dave led the group into the house and made the introductions. Chaun and Denise were setting the places at the dining room table. Michelle was placing all the dishes containing dinner on the table. Sara said, "Michelle, dinner smells amazing. You guys didn't have to cook dinner for us."

Michelle smiled, then looked at Sara. Michelle said, "Thank you. You guys are our guests for the evening. Granted, you're here to help us, but you are guests none the less. We always treat visitors in our home this well. We treat everyone invited through those doors as family."

Sara was awestruck. She was not used to such generosity and openness. Her jaw dropped. "That's very nice of you." Everyone sat down at the table. Dave and Chaun at either end with Denise and Michelle at their side. Sam's high chair was set between Michelle and Denise. The team sat on the opposite side of the table from Sam, Denise, and Michelle.

The family had prepared a lot of food for the evening. There were steaks, a few pork chops, mashed potatoes, green beans, corn, and fruit salad. After all their plates were fixed and everyone began to eat, Alex asked, "Have any other occurrences happened since we spoke on the phone yesterday?"

Dave shook his head, "No, it has been quiet."

Alex nodded. His voice sounded almost relieved. "Well at least that is some good news." He ate another bite of his steak. "How bad was the attack on Denise and Chaun the other night?" Since everyone had sat down at the table, Alex had been staring right at the cuts across the right side of Chaun's face. He motioned at Chaun's face with his fork. "Are those cuts from the other night?"

Chaun slowly nodded. "Unfortunately, they are. Denise's injuries were bad enough she needed seven stitches. After we are done eating, I'll show you the walls in my room and the jersey Denise was wearing."

Alex paused mid bite. He looked back at Chaun with a furrowed brow. "Was it that bad?"

Chaun nodded and looked at Alex with a non-threatening intensity. "The jersey is still stained. We could not get the blood out and there are two massive holes in two of my walls upstairs." Alex finished his bite of food.

Sara froze. Her mouth hung open. She exclaimed, "Wow! As far as the possession goes how can you tell if it's her or the person she is possessing?"

Dave answered, "The irises of the person she possesses turn dark black. When she leaves the person the black looks as if it turns into smoke and disappears into the pupils."

Sara took another bite of her food. She was still awestruck and mentally trying to process everything. "That's interesting. Is there anything else we need to look for to know if it is..." Sara looked at Dave for the answer of a name.

"Katrina."

"Thank you. ...Katrina or the person?"

"When the eyes are black the voice is high pitched, raspy, and hesitant." Dave looked at Gene. He was quiet and a little pallid. Dave's brow slightly raised. "Are you okay Gene?"

Gene nodded. His tone portrayed skepticism. "I think so, just a little nervous."

Alex then spoke, "It's his first investigation. He is still unsure whether or not the paranormal exists. He has decided to help us to gain an opinion on the issue."

Dave smiled and looked at Gene. "Well, if Katrina is active tonight, you will definitely have an opinion. I didn't believe in the paranormal myself until things started happening around here. You'll do fine. Don't worry too much. I don't think Kat will harm anyone tonight."

Gene nodded his head. He seemed to relax a little. The color also started returning to his face. He shook his head. "Everything you have been saying sounds so farfetched."

Dave took another bite of food and settled back in his chair. "I can see where it could appear that way. We've all been telling the truth."

Gene shook his head and raised his hands, palms out. "I meant no offense."

Dave smiled and shook his head. "None taken. Like I said, I didn't believe in the paranormal before all these events took place. I've seen things I can't explain. I've footage of something moving a camera from this table to that entertainment center on the other side of the room. I have seen items moved to that same entertainment center and stacked."

Alex's brow lifted with the pending question. "Have you figured out what message the items signified?"

Dave nodded, his look grew solemn. He raised his head and spoke. "Once I found out who was haunting the family it became a little clearer. The DVD stood for Katrina seeking payback for something that had made her feel wronged, the picture of the heart with broken glass stood for her heart being broken, and the clock, I can only assume, meant that she would be seeking revenge in her time."

Alex nodded as he took another bite. "That sounds like a logical line of thought. He looked around to Dave, Michelle, and Chaun. What kind of person was Katrina when she was alive?"

Dave answered. "To everyone else she was really sweet. To Chaun she was controlling and verbally abusive. She had to be the center of attention at all times and constantly had to have her way."

Alex's tone softened with his hesitance. "So she was extremely narcissistic?"

"Very. The longer she and Chaun were together the more we noticed that her being sweet to everyone was a façade. She was very conniving and manipulative."

Alex paused and looked down at his plate. "I see. Well if those personality traits make an appearance tonight, it should be an interesting night." The group finished dinner and the family began cleaning up and washing dishes as the group began to bring their equipment in from the van.

Chapter 28

Once all the equipment was moved into the house, Alex spoke with Dave. "Would you be able to walk us through the house and show us all the locations where all the activity has happened?"

Dave stepped to Alex's side. He placed his hand on Alex's shoulder. "I sure can." Standing at the foot of the staircase in the entryway, Dave pointed towards the living room. "You guys already know about the activity in the dining room and living room. After I show you around, I will show you the video footage."

Alex smiled ear to ear. "That would be awesome."

Starting up the steps, Dave said, "The most intense activity we've experienced was in the nursery and Chaun's room. We left the message on the wall. We figured the team would be interested in seeing it." As the group reached the top of the staircase, Dave walked through the door in front of the group. "This is Samantha's room." He motioned towards the wall to his left. "There's the message Katrina left for Chaun."

Alex, Sara, and Gene were all awestruck and speechless. In all the years Alex had been investigating the paranormal, he had never seen anything this extreme. Each of the letters was at least 18 to 24 inches long. "When you said there was writing on the wall, I pictured something smaller than this."

Dave nodded. His voice almost a whisper. "We noticed it in the dark."

Alex walked to the wall for a closer look. "I can believe it."

"Have you ever seen anything like this before?"

He shook his head. "Not as far as written messages go. Are you guys okay with us setting up cameras in here?"

Dave nodded then rubbed his mouth and chin with his hand. His behavior told Alex that the writing was not the only activity the family had experienced in the room. "That would probably be wise. The night this was written on the wall, we entered the room to find Sam sitting on the rail of her crib with her feet laced between the slats. She climbed down and stood in the crib. Most of the time, Sam is the one that Katrina chooses to possess."

Alex, Sara, and Gene traded glances between themselves. Alex then said, "Setting some equipment up in here would seem wise then wouldn't it?"

Dave just nodded. "If you all are ready, I'll show you Chaun's room." Alex nodded in response. Dave led the team out of the nursery. Once through the door, Dave turned left and escorted the team through the first doorway to their left. As soon as they entered, the team noticed the damage left from Denise's body. They walked over and inspected the wall across from Chaun's bed. Sara was the first to face the opposite wall. She faced Chaun's bed, and quickly covered her mouth with her hand. Alex turned and noticed that Sara was crying.

He placed his hand on her shoulder. His tone was full of worry. "What's wrong?" He followed her gaze to find the cause of her tears. His eyes locked on and followed trails of blood on the wall above Chaun's bed. They stopped, right before they reached the ceiling, at the hole made by Denise's head. His jaw dropped. "Holy shit! When you said she was lifted into the air, I thought you meant for a split second."

Dave shook his head. "No, she was dangling in mid-air above Chaun, while he was lying on the bed, for a few seconds. After that was when her head was slammed into the wall above the bed." He walked to the closet door and showed the team the jersey Denise was wearing during the attack. The front of the jersey looked as if it had been tie-dyed with blood. "This is what she had on at the time."

Alex looked at Dave in disbelief. "She didn't look like she had even been injured."

"It didn't cut deep, but even a small cut to the head will bleed profusely."

Alex nodded. "Good point."

Dave closed the closet door, then turned and looked at the group. He raised his hands then let them fall back at his sides. "That's about all the locations. There was some activity on the back patio, but that was when all of us were present. If you guys are ready, I can show you the video footage now."

Alex nodded. "That would be great. Thank you."

Dave escorted the team back down to the first floor. When he reached the bottom of the staircase he turned left into the study. He walked over to his computer and brought up the two videos he had captured from the dining room and living room. "This is the first of the two. It shows all but one of the entries into the dining room. No one enters the room and Denise never left the couch."

The team was amazed at the footage. Gene was still skeptical at the footage. "How do we know that someone wasn't standing behind the camera the entire time, or came in through the entrance not shown?" Alex looked at him for a second, and then focused his attention back on the screen.

Alex then spoke, "There is a reason why that is not a person moving the camera. A person could not lift a camera off the table and walk it across the room without jostling it at least the slightest bit. As far as the unseen entrance, no one can be seen leaving the room."

Dave looked at Gene. He closed out of the first video. "That's why I filmed a second night, just in case anyone had any doubts." Dave double clicked on the icon to access the footage of the three items being moved. "This was filmed the next night. I strapped the camera down to the dining room table so it would not be moved. This is what I captured."

Alex and Sara watched excitedly as they saw the items being moved to the entertainment center from different areas of the room. Gene continued to watch, mentally questioning how the family was able to manipulate the footage. Gene usually was questionable and tried to find reasoning in anything new that he could not explain. A lot of people do not believe in the paranormal. Gene was one of those people.

Alex looked at Gene. His face curled into a smirk. "Does that make you any more of a believer?"

Gene laughed. "You know how I am Alex. I won't believe something until I see it or feel it."

Alex pursed his lips for a second while taking in Gene's opinion. "Fair enough." Alex looked at Dave. "Well I think we will get started on setting up. You said that some of the family may want to help with the investigation?"

Dave's voice rose. He nodded. "Actually, Chaun and I definitely want to help. Denise is leery about helping due to the attack. She is scared that something may happen to her again. Michelle is willing to help watch cameras and footage if need be."

Sara nodded, then looked at Dave. Alex said, "We can accommodate that. Sara usually watches from inside the van on investigations. Just one more question though before we get started. No one in the family has heard any growls or seen any apparitions with animal heads, have they?"

Dave got a look of confusion on his face. "No, just the possessions, attacks, writings, and items being moved. Why do you ask?"

Alex traded a glance with Sara, and then looked back at Dave. "Usually when the activity includes growling and apparitions with animal heads, it's typically demonic."

Dave's brows almost met his hair line. He pursed his lips. "Oh, well I guess it's a good thing we haven't experienced that type of activity."

Alex smiled. "Well if you're ready, I think we can set up a camera in the dining room, Sam's room, Chaun's room, and the hallway. I wouldn't mind putting a radio or voice recorder in Sam's room."

Dave shut his computer down and stood up. "That sounds like a good idea."

The group stepped out of the office and into the foyer. Dave proceeded to help the team haul the cases of equipment upstairs and get it set up. Dave helped Alex set the camera up in the corner of the nursery adjacent to the door. This enabled the team to view the entire room and whether or not anyone was entering or exiting the room.

The crib was very close and completely visible through the camera lens. Alex communicated with Sara on his cell phone. She was in the van making sure all the camera angles were perfect. Once completed with their set up in the nursery, they continued to Chaun's room to set up the camera for that room. They placed the camera on the nightstand.

From this vantage point, like the nursery, the entire room was visible. Alex and Dave then returned to the nursery to set up the audio equipment. Within a few minutes, Sara said she could clearly hear what was going on within the room. Dave and Alex then returned to the first floor and set up the camera in the dining room. They placed it where all entryways and the entire living room could be seen by Sara, Michelle, and Denise in the van.

Alex said, "Are we ready for lights out?"

Sara answered, "Almost, Michelle has to get Samantha to sleep. Then, we will be ready."

Alex then went out to the van with Dave and Gene. He notified everyone present what they needed to look for during the investigation. "I usually don't prefer more than two people in the house at a time, but since I'm the only person with experience, all four of us will stay together during the investigation."

Chaun spoke, "That sounds like a plan. I'm pretty sure that there will be a greater chance of activity tonight if I am present." Being unsure of what to expect, he gave a nervous smile.

Chapter 29

After Michelle had taken Sam upstairs and got her to sleep, Alex and the others made their way up the stairs to Chaun's room. Due to the most severe attack happening there, Alex decided that would be the best room in which to start the investigation. Once in the room Alex pressed the record button on his digital recorder.

Chaun looked curiously at Alex. "Can you really pick up voices on those things?"

Alex nodded. "That you can," He set the recorder down at his side. "sometimes really clearly."

"Hmm…that's really interesting."

"Yes, it is." Alex paused for a second. His face asking before the words were uttered. Chaun's eyes and his locked on each other. He asked, "Would you be able to walk me through what happened the night of the attack?"

Chaun nodded, then looked at the floor a moment gathering up his memories of the order of events before speaking. "Yeah, I can do that." Chaun walked over to the same spot where he stood before climbing into bed that night, and started describing what had happened. He raised his arms in front of him, and then let them fall a few inches with the blades of his hands facing downward. "I was right in this spot. I stripped down to my boxer briefs and climbed into bed. I watched her while she stood by my closet undressing. Up until that point, I usually turned away when she did this, but that night was another story. I was ready to take things further. She caught me staring and we began flirting."

Alex nodded his head to let Chaun know he was listening. "She put on my jersey and climbed into bed. I told her that I loved her and we started making out. I was lying on my back when she straddled me. Her head suddenly jerked back, as if someone was pulling her hair. She was then yanked into the air."

Alex raised one of his hands to chest level. "When you say yanked into the air...?"

Chaun laid down on the bed and held his hand parallel, six inches above his waist in the air. "Her feet were here and she was hanging perpendicular to me and the bed. She was then thrown into the wall above the headboard. The next couple seconds, it was almost like someone was grabbing her hair and slamming her head into the wall. Her screams went silent and her body went limp after her head's second impact with the wall. She was then thrown across the room into the wall behind you. When mom and dad came in it felt like someone forcibly turned my head towards the door." He sat up. Chaun glanced at his bed for a moment and then, coming to another realization, back up at Alex. "I think that's when the lacerations were left."

Alex and Gene's mouths fell open. "Wow. How cold did it get in here when all this took place?"

Chaun shook his head and shrugged his shoulders. "We really didn't notice. When you are making out with someone your body doesn't think of cold. Her breath was visible right before her head was pulled back."

Alex nodded. "So, this attack didn't take all that long?"

Chaun shook his head. "Not long at all, only about 10 to 15 seconds, on the outside, no more than 20."

Alex nodded and interlaced his fingers. "What made you come to the conclusion that your former wife is the entity causing all the commotion?"

Chaun leaned against his headboard. "She spoke to me in a dream." He smirked and gave a slight laugh. "I know it sounds kind of farfetched, but it felt real."

He separated his hands, faced his palms up, and then interlaced his fingers once again. "What did she say or do in the dream that brought you to the conclusion of her being the entity?"

"Her eye color changed."

Alex's brow furrowed, "Changed how?"

Chaun's tone was hesitant. He was not sure how it would sound to someone other than family. "They started as her normal, brown eyes, and changed to the black orbs we've been plagued with the last few months." Alex nodded in response. "That's when I woke up and went downstairs to tell everyone."

"Well if that's the case, maybe we can try to communicate." Chaun nodded. Alex then spoke to the emptiness of the space surrounding the group. "Is your name Katrina?" He paused for ten to fifteen seconds. "Why are you here?" Alex paused again.

Dave became curious and asked, "Why do you pause after each question?"

"It is basically to give the entity time to answer." Dave's face portrayed confusion. Alex explained further. "An entity must draw excess energy to illicit a response."

"From where?" Dave asked.

"Electronic devices such as battery-operated items or an electrical appliance like a television."

Chaun squinted one eye. "How can you tell if it is drawing energy?"

"With a television you really can't tell, but battery powered equipment is another matter. A significant decrease in battery life usually precedes activity."

Dave nodded, "What do you mean by significant decrease?"

Alex looked at the recorder. "The battery, most often, will drop from a full charge to a half charge in a matter of seconds." The T.V. turned on. Alex looked at Chaun. He pointed at Chaun. "Did you do that?"

Chaun shook his head. "No." He pointed to the remote setting on the entertainment center. "That's the controller for it."

Alex stood up, walked over, and picked up the remote. Inspecting it he asked, "Has this happened before?"

Chaun shook his head. "No. This is the only time this has happened." Alex inspected the T.V. and found nothing out of the ordinary.

As he walked back over to his chair he said, "We can leave it on for now. Maybe she needs to gain strength to communicate."

Chaun laughed nervously. "Don't expect so little. Lately, she hasn't been much for subtle interaction." Unbeknownst to the group, while Alex and Chaun were talking, the connections were slowly being disconnected from the back of the T.V. When the power cord was removed from the outlet, the T.V. screen went black. Everyone turned their eyes to face the screen.

Alex raised his brow. In a joking tone he said, "Guess she doesn't feel like communicating." Chaun tensed as every hair on his arms and neck stood on end. Chaun's statement and reaction to the T.V. cutting out was validated a moment later. The Television lifted vertically off of the entertainment center. It stopped four feet above the floor and began floating in a semi-circle around the room. The set moved over Chaun and his bed, past Dave, and stopped across from Alex. As he watched the levitating appliance, he questioned what would happen next. Alex barely had enough time to dive out of the path of the set as it bolted towards him. The screen exploded as the T.V. slammed into the wall.

Within the next few moments, it sounded to the group as if, every door within the house was being opened and slammed shut repeatedly. Gene said, "Screw this!" He stood up and ran from the room. Alex, Dave, and Chaun left the room and ran after him.

Chapter 30

Alex caught up with Gene at the base of the stairs, with Dave and Chaun on his heels. "Gene. Hang on a second." Gene stopped with his hand grasping the knob of the front door. Alex leaned against the door. Alex made eye contact with Gene. He could tell Gene had just received the scare of his life. His eyes were glazed over and his face was pallid. "You okay?"

Gene's face started to gain a redder tint. "Hell no, I'm not okay."

Alex's voice softened. "Look, you believe in the paranormal now. Granted, you've witnessed something that typically isn't seen too often, but I still could use your help. I know you're freaked out right now. Hell, I would be too if that was my first experience with the paranormal."

Gene's brow furrowed. "No shit!" His brow rose. "How the hell are you so calm right now?"

Alex smirked. "Adrenaline and years of experience. Come on, let's go to the living room and all of us can sit and talk for a bit." Gene reluctantly nodded and followed Alex and the others into the living room. After the group was in the living room and everyone had sat, the group remained silent for a couple minutes. Alex looked at Dave. "How long did you serve in the military?"

Dave let out a sigh and leaned back in his chair. "A long time, 25 years. I made a full career out of it."

Alex looked at the floor and then back up at Dave. "That's awesome. What did you do in the military?"

Dave chuckled. "I was actually a cook my entire career, during my service and after my retirement."

"That's great."

Chaun was looking Alex over from a distance, with a concerned expression. "You sure you're okay? The T.V. didn't hit you at all did it?"

Alex briefly checked for blood or scratches. "I'm good. It missed me, only barely, but it still missed."

With an apologetic tone, Chaun said, "I had no idea that anything that extreme was going to happen."

"It's okay. Believe me, I've seen worse."

Chaun's eyes narrowed. "What do you mean by worse?"

"Well, actually I've seen worse than the attack you experienced upstairs."

"How could it get worse?"

Alex looked at the floor, his voice quieted, and his expression grew dark and distant. "Someone that was possessed actually laughed while every other person in the room was being held against the ceiling. Another time, a group member was thrown out of a window on the fourth floor of an apartment complex." The color drained from Chaun's face. "The person didn't survive the fall."

Chaun slowly nodded and spoke with a quiet reflective tone. "It sounds like Denise got off lucky."

Alex just nodded in response with a distant look in his eyes. "That's why I wanted to help you and the family out as soon as possible. If you guys were already experiencing attacks, to that extreme, it wouldn't be long before they started getting worse."

"Thanks again for coming to help us. I'm grateful that you made our situation a priority."

Alex shook his head and responded. "You don't need to thank me. I investigate to help people find answers and, if possible, resolve issues." As Alex spoke, steam from his mouth became more predominant. The temperature in the room had dropped drastically. Alex began visually looking around the room with a heightened sense of urgency. "Here we go again boys."

A stillness settled over the room for the next few moments. Alex and Chaun made eye contact. Alex's eyes were a light earthy hazel. In the millisecond it took for Alex to blink, his eyelids lifted to reveal two black orbs.

#

Alex helplessly watched as his head looked around the room. He realized he was not alone within his mentality. Within his thoughts he began speaking with Katrina.

What are you wanting Katrina?

Alex could feel her hatred. *I want him to suffer. I want him to feel pain.*

He thought with a sense of calm hoping it would ease her hostility. *He has felt pain.*

Not as much as I want him to.

Not realizing the internal conflict going on within Alex, Chaun spoke, "Katrina, leave him. Why are you hurting other people when I'm the one you want to hurt?"

Alex's face stretched into a grin that seemed wider than physically possible. "Chaun, I know how much you care about other people and put their needs and care above your own. That's the reason for hurting others. It hurts you more that I hurt others instead of you."

Chaun sprang to his feet and leaned over Alex. He hissed, "I wish you would stop." His voice began to raise. "You were always mean and controlling while you were living. Why I thought that you could now be more heartfelt and genuine, I don't know." His tone spiteful. "Oh, that's right, you have no beating heart." He stood up and said with a condescending tone, "Hell, I'm shocked you haven't been roaming the house whaling like a banshee. Your voice was that fucking annoying while you were living."

Alex pleaded with Katrina. He heard her thoughts and did not want to witness what she was about to do. Don't do this Katrina. Please don't do this.

Her mental tone utterly pissed and sadistic. Don't you see, I have to, even though I am no longer living, I still have complete control.

Alex watched as his body stood. Within the span of a second, Katrina placed Alex's left hand on Chaun's chest and pushed him back down into the chair so hard the momentum almost up ended the chair. She made her way towards the kitchen. Gene remained seated on the couch. He was too scared to move. Alex looked on, unable to take control of his body, as Katrina walked into the kitchen and grabbed one of the knives out of the block on the counter. She turned and slowly made her way back into the living room. She walked behind the couch and stood directly behind Gene. He attempted to get off the couch and distance himself from Katrina.

Alex watched in horror as Katrina grabbed a handful of Gene's hair with his left hand. She jerked hard enough that Alex felt some of Gene's hair break free of his scalp. Once he was back in a seated position on the couch, Kat continued to pull his head back exposing his neck. She placed the blade of the knife on Gene's neck. Katrina showed Alex memories of a tiny set of hands, knives, and numerous animals with their throats being slit. With each image the sickly, sweet, metallic scent of blood grew stronger. Kat's mental tone was a hiss dripping with pride. You see Alex, I was able to

236

control my urges growing up. I learned how to suppress them for the longest time. I gained control over those urges.

Within his mind, Alex was mentally pleading with Katrina. His mental tone almost a whisper. Please don't do this. All the others could see of the struggle raging within the recesses of Alex's mind and body were the tears streaming down his face.

Chaun watched as a trickle of blood began running down the back of Gene's neck. He heard the dripping of his blood hitting the hardwood floor behind the couch. Katrina spoke, her words slow and calculated. "You see Chaun. I always had control and I will always have control. When I was little, I used to do this to animals all the time. It's a secret I've kept for so many years."

Chaun was furious. His mental state edged close to the level it had the night of the accident. He yelled at Katrina. "Look, he has done nothing to you! Take the knife away from his neck and leave him alone!"

Alex's body stood up straight. Kat's eyes never leaving Chaun's. She pulled the knife away from Gene's neck and let go of his hair. A clump of his hair remained in Alex's hand. With a flick of Alex's arm, she flung the knife towards the floor, imbedding it an inch into the hardwood. "Fine. I'll leave everyone alone for now. I need to recharge for the next round anyways." Alex's face grinned again menacingly. Alex's hazel eyes reappeared with a blink of his eyes. Other than Gene's sobbing from the couch, the room was once again quiet.

Chapter 31

Michelle, Sara, and Denise watched in silent terror. Their hands covered their mouths holding in the silent screams of horror that wished to escape. They were speechless and petrified. No one moved or made a sound for many moments after Alex had stepped away from Gene. Holding the walkie-talkie in front of her mouth, Sara broke the silence, "Alex, what's going on?"

His voice answered back weak and shaky, "Give me a few minutes."

Looking at the picture streaming from the living room she nodded. "Okay, talk when you're ready."

Michelle, Sarah, and Denise saw Dave get up and leave the room. He came back a few minutes later with a bottle, four glasses, and a rag for Gene's neck. He handed each person in the room a glass and then poured whiskey into each glass. The four sat and sipped at their glasses for the next ten minutes. After it had appeared Gene had calmed a bit and the guys had talked, Alex came out to speak with Sara and Michelle. As soon as the van door opened, she could tell that he had been crying. Michelle spoke, "Is everyone okay?"

"Gene's not. He has a nick on his neck," Denise jumped out of the van and ran into the house to tend to Gene. "…but that pales in comparison to his emotional trauma. We just now got him calmed down enough for me to be able to step out to talk with you. This will probably be his last investigation." Sara climbed out of the van and hugged Alex.

Michelle said, her tone apologetic, "If you guys leave, we will fully understand. I don't want your team to be in more danger than it needs to be." She shook her head as tears fell. "We had no idea Kat would be this hostile to people just coming into the house asking questions."

Alex reached out and placed his hand on Michelle's shoulder. "We'll stay a little longer, but I can't promise we will find a solution."

Michelle nodded as she said, "I agree. Maybe with some of the things you've shown us about communicating we can solve the problem within the next few weeks or months." Through her peripheral vision, Michelle caught movement on one of the cameras.

It was coming from the nursery. She looked over just as Sam stood up in her crib and began climbing out. "Alex, quick, get to the nursery. Sam's climbing out of her crib."

As Alex burst through the front door and bolted up the stairs two at a time, the four in the living room stood up. Chaun and Dave ran for the staircase. Chaun yelled as he ran, "What's wrong Alex!?" Gene and Denise followed. Reaching the base of the stairs, they saw Alex at the top, facing down the hallway and not moving. He was frozen in place. When they reached the top of the staircase Alex stepped to the side to allow them room. The cause for Alex's lack of movement became known when they looked down the hallway and saw Sam standing, unaided with her arms at her sides, in the middle of the hallway. The glass on the window at the end of the hall and the wall sconces were frosted over. Sam looked like she was exhaling fumes from dry ice.

That eerie, recognizable voice emanated from Sam's mouth once more, "Hello Chaun. Ready for round two?"

Exasperated, Chaun said, "What will it take to end this? If I felt the pain you felt that night? Would that solve it?"

Sam's brow leveled. "Yes, it would. I want you to feel the pain I felt that night. The only way I can see fit to make you feel that pain is for you and others around you to be helplessly tormented."

Chaun shook his head. "Kat, you were so close to the solution at the beginning of all this."

Sam's right eyebrow lifted. Thinking Chaun was being condescending, she spat, "What do you mean?"

Chaun's tone was mellow. "Remember possessing the Chaplain at the hospital? He felt your anguish and feelings from that night. It's simple, possess my body and give me the alertness you gave him while with him."

Sam's brow rose in the center as her lips pursed, "You're right. I should have thought of this from the beginning."

Chaun held up his left hand toward the nursery. "Would you please put Sam back in her crib before we continue? I know you don't want her hurt."

Sam nodded, walked towards the group, turned, and walked into the nursery. Everyone watched as Sam slowly levitated off the floor, over the rail, and finally sank into the crib where she would be safe. Chaun watched as the eyes faded from black to green. As soon as the eyes changed, he noticed another presence within his mind. The other men watched as the eyes had changed. *Hello Chaun.*

The men could hear Chaun speaking aloud to Kat, "Hello Katrina." He turned and began walking down to the living room once again. Kat had already read his thoughts and allowed him the time to get downstairs and situated. She now realized, she could not allow him to be seriously injured due to his being Sam's only living parent. Once in the living room and seated, Chaun said, "I'm ready."

The replay of the accident played in his head, but this time seeing what Kat had seen and experienced that night. He felt her frustration and anger towards him. When the words were spoken, he felt Kat's feelings from that night. After hearing the words that emanated from Chaun's mouth her heart sank. How could he leave her after eight years of marriage? She had felt the cold insecure feelings that come with being disrespected and belittled by the person she cared for most in life. Someone she should have been able to trust. As she spoke within Chaun's mind, her voice was soft and sad. *Now you see. I love you and you treated me that way and made me feel like I was nothing.*

Chaun's brow furrowed and his tone was penitent. "I'm sorry I made you feel that way. Now, stay a little longer, I have something to show you." Visions started passing through his mind. Memories of what had transpired throughout their marriage. The first was memories of meeting her in the coffee shop and his peaceful joy seeing her reading among the trees. "You see, I was happy," His voice turned sorrowful. "up to a point."

Then, he began showing her the negative memories. They were taken back to a store checkout lane. She felt his emotions and saw through his eyes. While in the checkout lane she kept slamming the cart into him the whole time yelling at him that he was stupid and annoying. She looked on as Chaun looked at the cashier, an older woman with grey hair. Her eyes showed pity and sorrow. They were also questioning, "Why are you with her?" Chaun raised his eyebrows, paid, and then they left. She felt the same feeling he had experienced in her memory of the accident, only it was so much more intense. She had belittled him and made him feel so insecure and small. Katrina felt his ego and emotion constrict within him, and with it that cold feeling of embarrassment.

Katrina's tone was apologetic yet patronizing. "I'm sorry, but that was one time."

Projecting that it was finally his turn to speak, Chaun's voice rose in anger. "There's more." He then showed her a flashback of when his great uncle had passed. She was taken back to the hospital where he had visited alone after class one night. His Uncle was hooked up to an IV, heart monitor, and had tubes down his throat. She saw as Chaun broke down in his failing attempts to be strong for his uncle. Kat experienced that deep, caring, heartfelt emotion that Chaun felt for all his family members. Chaun then took her to a night after the Uncle's passing when Chaun sat by a window, curled into a ball, and crying while staring into the blackness of night on the other side of the glass.

The entire time Kat was badgering him and not showing any compassion for the person who was supposed to mean the world to her. Already weakened and vulnerable, he once again felt the embarrassing feeling of betrayal. This time it cut deeper than the incident in the store. His tone softened. "You see, the night you died, you felt what I had been feeling our entire marriage. I've got one more memory to show you, and it will give you my thoughts, emotions, and reasons for certain behaviors."

The next memory was of the party. She snapped. *Did I do something to upset you that night?*

He responded with patience. "Yes."

Chaun could sense her rising tension. It was almost to the point when she usually stopped allowing him to speak. *What?*

He remained calm and spoke with an even tone. "Give me a few minutes and I'll show you. She watched that night play out in Chaun's mind: his talk with Jake, her interrupting his conversation, and the fighting in the car. The entire time his thoughts were of being fed up and his unhappiness with the marriage. She could feel that he loved her with all his heart, but he was tired of being unhappy and not treated the way he deserved.

His mental voice remained flat and even. He spoke as if he had been talking to a child. "The blowup that night was not due to work and the frustration of interrupted conversation. It was an explosion of all the pain and frustration I had experienced at your hand. I couldn't take it anymore. You were always self-centered and never thought much of anyone else or their feelings and emotions.

The pain you felt that night, was how I felt the majority of our marriage."

Chaun felt her quietness. He realized that she was remorseful and sad, because she had caused him so much pain. Her voice was soft and sheepish. I'm sorry Chaun. I didn't know. Can you forgive me for all the wrong I've done?

Chaun's tone became lighter. "Of course, I can forgive you. I love you and always will. Can you forgive me for my blow up that night?"

"Yes, I can." Her agitation vanished. She seemed calmer and more at ease than she had been in the last years of their marriage. "So, things are good between us now?"

"Yes, they are, but I also think you need to apologize to everyone else, especially Gene." He paused as if listening, then looked at Gene. Gene, still being on edge from the attack, recoiled. "She is wondering if it is okay to possess you in order to feel what you felt while experiencing what happened earlier? She wants to say she's sorry, but to better understand, she wants to experience the pain you felt."

Gene paused for a few seconds and then nodded. Inside Chaun's head she was still communicating for a few more moments. Chaun could sense her fear building as she thought, *Since everything is good now, does that mean I'll have to leave?*

"No Kat. You don't have to leave, as long as you don't cause harm to anyone ever again."

Deal. In a light-hearted, mischievous tone she thought, *can I at least pull pranks on people once in a while? What's the point of being a ghost if I can't freak people out?*

Chaun laughed, "That's fine. I want you to apologize to Denise as well."

I will.

Chaun felt solitude once again within his mind. An instant later, Gene's eyes were looking around with black orbs.

Epilogue

After that day, conditions improved around the house. Everything seemed more peaceful and Katrina kept her word. Some of the pranks she started pulling were pretty hilarious. She only possessed Sam a handful of time from that day forward.

Chaun paid for all of Gene's therapy. Due to the therapist not believing him, the poor guy had to actually take the video footage in of some of the occurrences that happened. First, he showed the knife being held to Gene's throat and then the footage of the TV being thrown and Sam levitating back into her crib.

After seeing the footage, the therapist took the footage to the prosecuting attorney, who then had Alex arrested for threatening bodily harm with a deadly weapon. The instance went to court where Chaun, Dave, and Gene testified in Alex's defense. All the footage of the investigation was shown to the courtroom. The judge and prosecuting attorney dropped the charges after the judge jumped up and started dancing in front of the entire courtroom. The entire time with black eyes he was chanting, "Who's a sexy girl? I'm a sexy girl!" Immediately after his eyes changed color, he called counsel into his chambers and dismissed the case. Dave and Chaun were in tears laughing.

Katrina, from that day forward, never showed any hatred towards Denise. In reality, and as oddly as it sounds, the two grew decently close. The way they would converse was Kat possessing Denise. In the beginning they mostly discussed Chaun. Conversing through thought, they would talk about Chaun's mannerisms and certain aspects that both thought cute or admirable. Two years later, Chaun and Denise were married. It was a small wedding, held in Dave and Michelle's back yard. Dave was Chaun's best man and Sam was the flower girl.

Alex, Sara, and Gene kept in touch with the family and the group became very close. Even though the first investigation he went on scared him into therapy, Gene continued to investigate with Alex and Sara. Alex told him that most paranormal investigations never went to that extreme. Usually they would only see furniture move or capture voices on the recorders. With this in mind Gene was more at ease to experience the less intense investigations.

Katrina acted as protector over Samantha and the family. Those visiting or at the house on friendly terms she never hurt again.

There were a few other times when she got physical with someone threatening harm to one person or another from the family, but those can be written down and told at a later time.

Katrina and Sam grew to have a good relationship. Granted it was hard for Sam when she was younger to not discuss her relationship with Katrina while at school. Bullies never messed with her for long. They would usually have harmless accidents that would cause them to become victims of bullying themselves.

I know and am writing all of this after years of having these stories told to me. I have heard them since I was young. Katrina is still present with the family and makes an appearance every once in a while. She has assisted me in the finer details of this story. Katrina, Chaun, Denise, Dave, and Michelle: I love all of these people dearly. I am Samantha Hutchins. I have grown to love Denise like I do my own mother. She has never treated me with indifference compared to my other siblings. I still love Katrina. I always will.

Dear Reader,

Thank you for your support! I truly hope you enjoyed the story. If you would like to follow updated news on any upcoming projects go to www.aaronbrinker.com for updates on future projects or some of my recommended reads.

Reviews go a long way for Authors. If you would be so kind as to leave a review with your thoughts over Second Chances, it would big a huge help in letting me know what you enjoyed and areas that I can improve to pen a more enjoyable read in the future.

Kindest Regards,

Aaron D. Brinker

www.ingramcontent.com/pod-product-compliance
Lightning Source LLC
Chambersburg PA
CBHW051236250626
47155CB00009B/3053